CATRINA BELL

Beastly & Bookish

HORNED UP FOR THE HOLIDAYS
a Winter Bliss Romance

The story, all names, characters, and incidents portrayed in this production are fictitious. No identification with actual persons (living or deceased), places, buildings, and products is intended or should be inferred.

Book Cover Illustration by Lana @redhead_trickster

Book Cover Design by Catrina Bell

Illustrations by Brina Boyle (map, page 100), Daniel Toro (page 173), Luna Wolff (page 200), Sali's Illustrations (page 233), H Holden (page 249)

Editing by Owl Eyes Proofs and Edits

First edition 2023

Contents

*To my book-loving grandmas
who made a book-loving me:
I love and miss you every day.*

*To the bookish community:
Thanks for the friendship, the laughs,
and the good (but also very, very bad) recommendations.*

Winter Bliss
& Surrounding Area

Chapter One
Rom

"**A** deal's a deal, Jaromar. The building is yours."

The older demon and I clasp forearms in a traditional handshake. My eyes glow fever-warm while his burn a brighter shade of red. We nod at the same time, sealing the agreement.

Demonkind are natural bargainers and will con you out of the clothes on your back, but when we make a deal, we stick to it. There's no one I understand better and would rather do business with than my own kind. While we're the least populous of the world's people groups, here in Winter Bliss, we're the majority. The active volcano nearby is an epicenter for demons who come for the holidays and to ski the lava flows that erupt every winter.

The real estate agent, Balthazar Jones, leans back and surveys the empty storefront he just rented me. "My Maggie will love having a coffee shop in this old building. What're you naming the place?"

"Perkatory."

"Ha! Glad to see the Perchaz family doing so well." He's an old friend of my dad's, and a grin kicks up on one side of his face at the name. Perkatory is a play on words, not only nodding to our family name but our demon background too, at least the human myths about us ruling some hellish purgatory full of fire and brimstone.

Call me crazy, but it always sounded kind of pleasant.

My family started the business as a coffee cart at the local university in Austin, Texas. Mom and Dad manned the mobile drink stand while us kids ran deliveries all over campus. That single rickety cart grew into a fleet of coffee trucks then brick and mortar locations. Business has never been better. Between my parents and brothers, we manage a flagship cafe, a roastery, and four chain locations throughout Texas. Big families are common with fated mate couples, like my mom and dad.

This lease in Idaho will be our first expansion as a national brand. And choosing a sleepy holiday town like Winter Bliss is no coincidence. It's where I spent the glory days of childhood.

Out the lead-paned front windows, sit the general store and post office, as quaint as ever. Closer to my heart, this empty storefront is next door to the town library, my favorite place as a kid.

Maybe she's still here somewhere, my mind whispers.

I peek at the older demon as I gather the paperwork set on the glossy bartop. He would know. But how do I ask without him looking too hard into it? Demons, especially demons in a small town like this, gossip like it's everybody's business.

And I've always hated being the center of attention.

"How is your wife?" I ask. They lived on the same street as *her* family back then.

"The woman never stops working." He beams. "Started an Etsy shop that sold like hot cakes and helped us buy our dream home, a new chalet up on the BZB."

"Nice."

Well, damn. He moved to the rich mountain down the road. Mount BZB is a snowy paradise of a mountain compared to its twin closer to town, the fire-scarred and treacherous ridges of Mount Winter Bliss. Only the wealthiest locals can afford to live near the luxe five-star resort and hobnob with the mega-rich tourists.

Good for him. At the same time, there's no inroad to press him about his old neighbors. My childhood best friend. *What if she's still here?*

His phone dings. When he looks down, his eyes light up, and a familiar flush colors his face, which for a demon can only mean one thing. A deal is going down.

"Gotta run to another appointment, son."

It's the demon way. Make money and chase the bottom dollar. Bargain for the lowest price so we can reap the highest profit. It's a compulsion. An instinct. A tickle in the back of our mind when the opportunity to gain an advantage presents itself. Because of our unique nature and competitiveness, demons dominate the business world.

And I've never fit in. I mean, I'm good at business. Really good, in fact. But my motto? Work smarter, not harder.

Today for instance, I used the flight from Austin to Boise to file the small business paperwork with my lawyer. After some targeted market research, I selected the three best storefront vacancies with availability to tour today. The first was the best, and within an hour of arriving in Winter Bliss, I have the keys to our new space. I didn't bother to haggle on the rent much beyond the customary two counteroffers. Frankly, we got a killer deal. While the real estate market in this small town is hot, it's still pennies on the dollar compared to what I'd have paid.

As Balthazar leaves, I exhale and look around the barren space. New electrical and roof. A decent kitchen area. It's an empty shell, but the exposed brick walls and a century-old vintage bartop are great bones to build the Perkatory aesthetic upon. I can see it now. Gothic light fixtures, richly tufted seating, and a long wall of bookcases.

The best part of our business, in my opinion, is the lending library. Mom and Dad don't love my insistence on lining every available wall with used books available for free. *It's bad business. We should stock merchandise. At least sell new books at retail price, Jaromar.* I understand the argument, but it's the only thing I put my foot down about as their general manager.

And if my calculations are correct, we'll be in the black on Perkatory's newest location within six months. But first, we have to get the coffee shop up and running, and to do that I'm stuck here until my mom's second cousin gets back into town. She'll be the store manager, and I want to make sure she's set up for success before I leave the launch logistics in her care.

I twirl the keys on my finger and pocket them, congratulating myself for a hard day's work completed in half the time. I click two buttons on my phone and "Out of Office Activated" grays out the screen.

Is there anything better than two weeks off with nothing to do except read books? The answer is, most definitely, no.

Leaving Perkatory's newest location, I feel like a king.

Two hours later, trudging through gray slushy ice as I cross the street, I feel more like a fool.

I can't find a hotel room to save my life, and every vacation rental online is booked. This town has seen a glow-up I wasn't expecting! There are cheery holiday decorations, fancy streetlights, and the sidewalks are clean and completely clear of snow. A featherlight flurry swirls around but nothing sticks to the ground.

"Rom?"

I look up. No one calls me that except close friends.

The bearded ugly mug of a demon, more mountain monster than man, blinks at me. Then I notice the unique shadow of hazel orange-black eyes and familiar scowl. Even years later, it can only be—

"Azgoran?" I rear back and shake my head. His hair is messy and clothes unkempt. "Damn dude, you look . . ."

He grimaces. "Like shit? Yeah, it's been a tough couple years."

"Huh." I scrub a hand down my face. "Mom heard through the grapevine you came into some money. Figured you'd be living large." Maybe it was a rumor or he lost it gambling. It happens.

He shrugs and grumbles something incoherent, turning to walk away.

"Hey!" I say, a little miffed he's just walking away.

He turns back.

"You know why all the hotels are booked up?"

His head juts forward, expression telling me I'm an idiot. He gestures toward the blackened active volcano towering over the valley. "Winter Bliss go boom."

I pause. Think about the date. We're right around the holidays. "Oh, shit. New Year's Eve."

"You really forgot?" He looks at me with a hint of a smile that's also a little sad. From the winter solstice to the new year, the holidays were some of the best days of our childhood. Visitors and locals alike packed the streets for the parade and festival, ending with a midnight party on New Year's Eve in the town square. Demons from all over converge on this sleepy town to take part in a fire-magic ritual to conjure Mount Winter Bliss to erupt. It's a long-held tradition to ensure the active volcano lets off some steam and stays safe for another year.

There was no shortage of trouble my brothers and I got into over the winter school breaks. Skinny dipping in Teapot Lake. Jumping over campfires without our clothes catching. Sneaking extra food samples from the holiday market vendors.

"I guess I just lost track of the days." I shake my head and gesture to my much older, rounder body. "Or more like the years."

He chuckles.

"Damn," I say. "I was looking forward to checking out the town, maybe seeing who's still around." A vision of a girl with fire-bright hair haunts me again. Az seems like a loner. It's probably safe to ask. "Say, you remember Noelle?"

His gaze narrows. "The librarian?"

"Yeah, his niece."

"No. She's the librarian now."

I stand straighter, then glance down the road to the storefront I leased just next door to the historic library. My heart races, blood roaring in my ears. I run a hand over the metal covering my broken horn and tug the hair on the right side of my face further down to cover my scars. Smoothing down my sweater, I realize how rumpled it is. I look like shit, but stopping by the library is now at the top of my to-do list once I find a place to freshen up.

"You know a place I could stay?" I ask.

He considers me for a moment, then smiles. "Remember Old Ethel?"

"The lady that used to tase us when we tried to steal candy at her corner store?"

"Same one. Still there too. She owns a cabin up Last Hour Road that's definitely got no renters."

"I checked the apps," I say doubtfully. "Everything's booked up. You really think so?"

"I know so. Wanna bet?"

I smile. A demon, even one as miserly and rough around the edges as Az seems these days, can't resist a friendly wager.

"Nah. I trust you. Her customer service skills were never top notch."

"Some things never change."

I hand him my business card and lean over for a friendly shoulder pat on the left side as we say goodbye. I know how ugly I am and have grown used to hiding as much of the messed-up half of my face as possible.

Watching him go, I wonder what his story is, how a guy with millions in the bank could end up like this. It makes me even more curious what the town librarian is like these days, because if Noelle is still in town, I plan to bargain that old demoness for whatever she wants to get a cabin nearby.

What she wants is highway robbery.

Cash up front. Double the nightly rate of the best boutique hotel in town. And she insists I hire her son full-time with benefits for a two-year contract at the new Perkatory location. Apparently word travels fast, and she'd already heard about the lease.

The money is no problem. Double is better than triple, which was where she sat for the first half hour of our negotiation. But hiring Sneaky Simon? Hard pass. He was two years older than me in school and a crook to his bones. Some people can change, but I have my doubts about that dude.

Old Ethel snaps her fingers, and a blue flame dances to life at the tips of her nails. She lights the long black cigarette holder perched between her knobby fingers. All demons have fire magic but it varies just like our morphology. Horns, tails, fangs, wings, and more present in some demons and not others. They're determined by our ancestor clans and unique genetic code as those cultures clashed.

We *all* have fire powers, though. I could have lit that cigarette for her. The fact she did it herself means not only is our negotiation still active, but she's also keeping her cards close.

Her gaze cuts over me as she takes a deep drag, the embers on the end glowing a bright orange that nearly matches her eyes. Demons always run a hard bargain, but the older demonesses are the most cutthroat. I know what my mom would do right about now — another round of offers, perhaps circle back to raising the nightly cabin rate, anything to wear the other party down. Persistence pays off.

I can't show how exhausted this makes me, so I lean forward on the counter, keeping my fists tight and gaze steady. If she senses weakness, she'll drive me all the harder.

When she exhales, smoke curls out her nostrils like a living monster, sweetening the air and softening the deep grooves of her wrinkles.

"Hire Simon."

"No." My response is immediate. I don't mind paying double for a two-week stay but hiring her son for a two-year contract? That's not gonna fly with our company's HR policies.

"No deal." She flicks her ash up in a delicate, silver arc and it turns to dust before it hits the laminate counter.

A light growl rumbles from my throat, and my jaw tenses. She smirks at me because I just betrayed how much I want this. It's up to me to compromise now.

"Why doesn't he work for you?" I ask, even though I know. I just want to hear it from her.

She sniffs and inclines her head. "Nepotism is a horrible thing."

I scoff. That's probably a dig at my family, but nepotism is the demon way. Demonkind trust our close family in business, while we keep everyone else at arm's length. But our new store manager is a tough cookie. She can keep him in line or cut him loose.

"I can offer a three-month probation employment. Benefits kick in if he passes the first evaluation at thirty days. If he performs, he can stay."

Her smirk is set in stone. I can't read her. The boundaries need to be clear.

"If he steals or does anything shady, he's out." I say. "Rules are rules."

Her red skin and eyes begin to glow, otherworldly. She's excited. An agreement is close.

"And fair is fair." Her voice is like honey. "So, we have a deal?"

I need that cabin, and now it's mine.

I count out the thick wad of cash required to pay for the cabin. Placing it in her hand, she drops a rabbit's foot keychain with a single antique key in my opposite outstretched palm. The address on the paper tag reads *972 Last Hour Road.*

I lean a little closer, eye level, and grasp her soft, wrinkled forearm, paying her the same respect as Mr. Jones for an agreement reached between two consenting parties.

My eyes warm, field of vision tinted a pinky haze.

Her face brightens, spidery veins glowing gold from under her thin, near-translucent skin.

We both nod and say together, "A deal is a deal."

She smiles, transforming her wrinkled face into something beautiful and sinister.

The front door clatters closed behind me.

"Oh, dear. I'm sorry to interrupt, Miss Ethel."

The demoness's sharp gaze snaps to the voice behind me, and her villainous smile turns soft.

"Noey, right on time."

I straighten and turn, fidgeting with the fall of hair on my right side so it's covering my scars. My heart pounds against my ribs, body flashing hot and hotter. My palm slips on the counter, and I bang my elbow. Sweaty in five seconds flat. Embarrassing.

Thank the Mother Below for the countertop holding me up.

Noelle Goode is a sight to behold.

I thought she was pretty when I was a teenager, but the woman before me is something else. She shakes out her hair, and the red strands blaze around her, lit fierce and breathtaking in the afternoon sun. Her pale skin is a healthy pink all over. Snowflakes stick to her shoulders and eyelashes like sprinkles on a cupcake.

She moves closer, speaking to the demoness behind me, but I hear nothing. My mind is buzzing. A hot instinct I've never felt before courses through my blood.

Is she real? The beautiful redhead moves so smoothly it's as if she's floating more than walking.

My body twists as she approaches the counter, turning so she only sees my left side, the decent half of my face. As she moves closer, chatting with Old Ethel, the side of her hand grazes mine.

"Oop. Sorry." She flashes me a smile before going back to her conversation.

My skin burns. My glasses fog up a little as I look her over. That's when I notice she's wearing roller skates.

I grin. How can I not?

As a kid, she was always on skates. Up and down the library stacks, she helped her uncle shelve books or popped down the street to run errands for him. I can still see the bruises and rainbow Band-Aids that covered her legs. Falling never scared her, even though her skin was more delicate than a demon's. She tried to teach me once with her strap-on skates. I was useless. In my mind, I can still hear her laugh at my halted attempt. But unlike the kids who used to tease me for my face or having a stutter, she never laughed at me. We laughed together.

I peek at her left hand, heart in my throat. Surely, she's married with a brood of kids.

Nothing. I exhale. Even her style is familiar. She always loved bright colors and still does judging by her bright puffer jacket and orange leg warmers. But adult Noelle is generously curved, filling out her clothes in the most voluptuous of ways.

The smile on my face must be maniacal at this point by the way I can feel it tugging on my scar. They say sparks fly when you meet someone special, and man is that right.

The tingly shock of electricity zaps my elbow.

"What the Holy Mother—" I rear back and glance at the old demoness waving her mini taser at me. "You tased me!"

"Miss Ethel, you know how the chief of police feels about you assaulting town visitors." Noelle chides.

"Shoo!" The older lady lunges forward, electricity crackling blue and white around her weapon of choice. To her, I'm just some nobody outsider eyeing Noelle up. As much as I don't enjoy being zapped with high voltage electricity, I can't help but respect her protectiveness.

"She doesn't mean any harm, sir." Noelle turns to me with an apologetic smile.

My mouth snaps shut.

She really doesn't remember me. This girl was my best friend until I moved away. My first crush. We shared every secret, but now she has no idea who I am.

Noelle slides a bright yellow flier and a paperback book across the counter toward the demoness. It's a plastic-covered historical romance with a vintage illustrated cover.

The hero is practically nude on the cover, holding a lady fainting in his arms. It looks so familiar. Oh wait—

"That's really valuable." I point to the book and pull up my phone to do a quick internet search. "Yep. $50 on the low-end. $100 or more for a signed first edition in like-new condition. It's an iconic and controversial book cover in the romance genre."

"Is that so?" Ethel looks over the book, front and back, with interest.

I can see the wheels turning already.

"It belongs to the library." I glare. "Better not go missing." She could report it lost, pay the list price, and resell it for higher. The old demoness smirks at me with a cocked eyebrow. *Yeah, I know how you work, lady.*

"Huh. Who knew?" Noelle looks at me again and squints. My heart is in my throat hoping she'll recognize me, but she simply shakes her head and turns back to Old Ethel. "Got a few more deliveries to make. Still raising money for the library."

"That's right." The older woman pockets the giant wad of cash I gave her and comes back with two wrinkly dollar bills and a lollipop.

"Ah, thanks." Noelle takes them with a smile, but it looks strained. Her disappointment is evident. "I'll bring you another steamy read next week."

"Same time, same place." Old Ethel picks up the book, her eyes dancing over the cover.

The neon flier slips further down the counter toward me. I pick it up.

FUNDRAISER! SAVE OUR LIBRARY!

FREE DELIVERY OF PERSONALIZED BOOK RECOMMENDATIONS.

DONATIONS GLADLY ACCEPTED.

CONTACT NOELLE FOR MORE INFO. 555-2116.

By the time I look back up, the door is swinging shut and Noelle skates down the sidewalk in a flash of red hair. I stride up to the front window, unable to take my eyes off her. Gosh, she's pretty. A woman on a mission. While there's a little snow in places, the sidewalks and road are mostly clear. At the stop sign, she crouches and rolls around the corner.

Gone from sight, just like that.

"Don't even think about it," the old demoness shouts. "I know that look, and I know that girl."

I turn back, patting my front pocket holding the key to my new place. A deal's a deal. Her cabin is mine for the next two weeks. Plenty of time to reconnect with a pretty librarian with fire-bright hair.

"You do, do you?" I know Noelle too, and this lady just cheaped out on her when she's trying to raise money for a good cause. I take that a little personally.

"Noey's a good girl." Her glower is a terrible thing. She picks up her long cigarette and takes a deep drag, eyes trailing over me dismissively. I know what she sees. Noelle would never go for me. I'm beastly, ugly as sin, whereas she's the town beauty. For a second, my confidence falters until Old Ethel flicks the ash off and stares me in the eyes. "She doesn't date outsiders."

That's it? This lady has no idea that Noelle and I knew each other. My brain tickles, neck and face flashing hot at the opportunity to prove her wrong.

I have zero game with women. Less than zero, actually, more like forty below and my nuts are freezing off. They take one look at my face and no matter my business success, it's a polite brush off. I shouldn't make this bet. My brain says walk away, but the demon instinct inside wonders.

What if it's possible?

I'd already planned to find a way to talk to Noelle, and some girls like scars, right? I'm far from confident and this is a stupid deal, but I lay my money on a losing bet with the fakest smile of self confidence I can muster.

"You wanna bet?"

Chapter Two
Noelle

Everything feels different when I'm skating. No one can catch me. Nothing can go wrong. I can accomplish anything I need to.

I pump my arms and skate faster, catching some real speed around the corner on my way back to the library. I know these streets like the back of my hand, and right now I'm flying, enjoying the smooth new blacktop of my charming hometown.

There are bad sides to frantic economic growth in a small town. Oversold hotels. Rising real estate prices. Increasing cost of, well, everything. But there are good things too, like improved roadways and heated sidewalks. There's some fancy tubing embedded under the concrete that keeps the pavement completely clear year-round. It's freaking a-ma-zing! I skate around for practical reasons — efficiency and health — but mostly I do it because it's fun, because kid Noelle would have died to roller-skate around town in winter.

The elites who retire to ski chalets on the BZB dominate our town council. They love to fund improvements to the aesthetic of the town square, anything in service of more tourist dollars.

Tourists like that demon in Miss Ethel's corner store. I don't know what it was about him that made me want to escape.

Okay, that's a lie. I do.

He unsettled me. He was so striking with his big shoulders, long fall of black hair, and delicate eyeglasses. *Swoon.* And the way his intense stare felt like a caress. *Double swoon.*

But every time I took a peek, there was something else. Something I couldn't put my finger on. Something *familiar.* It caught me off guard.

Do I know him from somewhere? Is he vacationing at the resort? With the polished style of his clothing, it wouldn't surprise me, but the way he and Miss Ethel interacted, so at ease, it was like he knew her, like he was a local.

No. I shake my head and skate faster. I know all the locals. I know the locals' family members who come into town for holidays. I know the vendors who stock our stores weekly. I've lived in Winter Bliss since the day I was born.

He's a tourist. Has to be.

And out-of-towners are off limits. They always leave. There's no point in flirting with a man who'll be on his way.

Some people can manage the smash-and-dash approach, but it's just not me. I've had enough heartache over the years. The first was my best friend when I was a kid. His family just up and left town one day, and I never heard from him again. Then, the boy I shared my first kiss with at sixteen ended up only staying for a brief stint at a local summer camp.

A string of short-lived flings followed, and then only a couple years ago, a demon swept me off my feet when he came into town trying to win it big at the resort's casino. He was the most charming man I'd ever met and so well-read. The only jackpot he won was cleaning me out of the $600 in my checking account before skipping town. Ouch.

I stay away from visitors now. No sense in hurting my own feelings, you know?

I slow my pace as I navigate an older, cracked section of pavement and run smack dab into someone.

"Oh, I'm sorry, sir," I say.

The demon is about my age with golden ombre horns that arch up in a tall, elegant curve. Pretty and uncommon. He's dressed to the nines in a cream cashmere sweater and shiny gold piercings through his eyebrow and ears.

"Stay to the right, and you won't run into people." He takes the time to thoroughly inspect his sweater for — I don't know — smudges or an imprint of me, I guess, before walking on without a backwards glance.

"Welcome to Winter Bliss," I mutter as I roll my eyes and skate on. He's *definitely* not from around here, almost certainly coming from the Emberlight Resort. The rich tourists that stay there are good for the local economy but snooty as all get out. My mind drifts back to the demon with glasses in the corner store who seemed so nice.

No, Noelle. I shake my head. *Don't go there. You don't date outsiders.*

As for dating locals? It's slim pickings in this sleepy town, I'll say that. If you like thrice-divorced layabouts or money-hungry gamblers or anti-social mountain men, you're set.

Me? I want something more.

I refuse to settle for good enough. I've seen too many of those kinds of marriages while skating up and down these streets my whole life.

Around the next corner, I find two demons hanging up a shiny banner across Main Street.

TRUTHFIRE FESTIVAL

Town Square - Sunset - New Year's Eve

"Hey, there! How're the twins?" I ask. The married demon couple work odd jobs for the city during special events, and their boys just turned four.

"Much better." The wife smiles down at me as her husband pipes in, "Rowdy and full of rage."

I laugh. "Firing on all cylinders then."

"Count us in for storybook circle on Saturday. Their four little cousins from out-of-town are comin' too."

"Oh, I bet they're so big now. Can't wait!" I grin, then immediately pause in front of the bakery and pull out my phone. With my recorder on, I whisper, "Storybook circle. Pick a book and find an extra staffer for the day."

Voice memos are the only way thoughts stay put and things get done. I review them every night before bed and make alarms to keep me on track. Life is hectic but good. I exhale and lean against the bakery's brick front column, giving myself just a moment to breathe. The scent of warm bread and sugary treats lifts my spirits a little.

Life has gotten busier than usual lately. Running our family's nonprofit library on my own with just a small staff of mostly volunteers has been a challenge. But the added stress of our financial woes is really weighing on me.

Not to mention, the holidays are coming up. Families and tourists are already trickling into town, bundled up in matching outfits and hugging on doorsteps. Wreaths and mistletoe hang in doorways. Candles, trees, and festive displays light up front windows. It's a week and a half until New Year's and whether the culture calls for seven, eight, or twelve days of holiday cheer, there's one uniting factor.

Everyone is celebrating, and everyone is welcome at the Truthfire Festival on New Year's Eve. It's the same night as an important demon winter holiday, and with so many of them in town, it's become a bit of a catch-all holiday event. There's entertainment, roaring fires, and plenty of good food to go around, anything that can be cooked over an open flame — cinnamon-infused cider, candied apples, roasted chestnuts — you name it.

As much as the sight of my hometown coming to life around the holidays brings me joy, it also leaves me feeling a little lonely. Mom and Dad are on a cruise this year, my uncle recently moved into a memory care facility down the street, and I'm an only child. I don't get homesick for my own family too often because I see everyone in Winter Bliss as my family. That is, until their real families show up in town, leaving me feeling left out.

"*Bonjour.*" The top half of the door next to me swings open and the town baker, a bright-eyed fae woman with mint green skin, leans out, her every movement as graceful as a swan.

"Oh, hello!" I shuffle through my bag and hand over her book delivery. She was in a reading slump, but I knew the perfect solution — a food journalist's gastronomic history of the diverse cultures in Zanzibar. "It's due back in a week or I can pick it up with your next personalized book delivery."

She eyes the bright photographs on the cover and nods while reading the summary on the back before setting it aside. "*Merci.*" She lifts a still-steaming pastry toward me with a $10 bill tucked into the artfully folded paper holder. "Hope this helps the fundraiser, *ma cherie, et le pain au chocolat* on the house."

"Thank you so much! Double thanks!" I beam at her, mouth watering. $10 is a sure sight better than Miss Ethel's tip, but I brush the thankless thought away. Every dollar helps and there's no time to catch up on reading like the holidays. My best fundraising days are ahead of me.

I may get wistful this time of year when everyone else is cuddled up with their families, and I'm still alone. But I'm not *that* lonely. I have a town full of people who care about me. That's not nothing.

I skate further down the street, finishing off my pastry in four big bites.

Winter Bliss is my home. Every building brings me so much comfort, but one building more than most. The two-story, historic library I live and work in.

Seeing the bright blue awning, a new addition, just a couple doors down, fills me with joy. It's a family thing. Over a century ago, my family started a reading room in the empty space and have managed it ever since. My uncle was the longest running town librarian. With over thirty years of service, he's my hero and mentor. But when he was diagnosed with early onset dementia at sixty last year, I took the reins.

Since I was a kid, I'd been his helper, and I just finished my master's in library science online. I was ready, even if the circumstances were bittersweet.

There's a lot weighing on my shoulders. Years of budget constraints and details slipping through the cracks of my uncle's memory means the building is in sad shape.

I've tried to get my arms around all the repairs we need, but there's only one solution.

The library has to move. Our building just has too much that needs to be done: a new roof, faulty electrical connections, and a shifting foundation, among about a dozen other issues.

At the last budget meeting, the town council denied my request to renovate the library using grant funds earmarked to historic buildings. As a privately owned public library, I guess we didn't make the cut. They chose to invest in making the town square facades pleasing to the eye instead of fixing structural issues. Tourists really only drive through our town to gas up or maybe have a meal on their way to and from the BZB's luxury ski resort.

Their message to me was simple: I have to make do.

Well, librarians are nothing if not resourceful.

"No rest for the cheery," as my uncle likes to say.

And in a town this small, we can start fresh right here. My fingers graze over the shiny new doorknob of the building next door to the library. I peer in. It used to be a soda fountain decades ago with a long wood bartop that would make a perfect circulation desk. Then it became an antique store. When that went out of business, the building sat empty for years. The owners renovated it and recently put it back on the market. It's only half the size of the library, so I'll have to downsize our physical book collection. Even thinking about getting rid of books makes me shiver with discomfort, but needs must.

It'll be a tight fit making the finances and the layout work, but I can do it. I nod my head. Cute and cozy. It'll be fine. The library will live on for another generation.

I may be getting ahead of myself though. The lease isn't mine. *Not yet.* I've been negotiating with the realtor on the monthly rental price. Demons love to haggle, and it's not my strong suit, but I'm hoping persistence pays off. My lease is up on New Year's Day, and I really think Balthazar Jones is about to crack. No one else has snapped up this building, and it's been on the market for months. He'll just *have* to lower the rent, right?

In two more strides on my skates, I squeak to a stop in front of the library. My breath fogs up the stained glass of the front window on a sigh. I trace a star, then a long swirly line up to the next candy colored pane. I have every inch of this place mapped and memorized in my mind. Leaving this old building will be painful. I can already feel emotion tightening my chest at the thought. But there's no money, too much to do, and no one else but me to do it.

We have to move, and this fundraiser has to succeed. We need movers, some furniture, and enough to cover first and last month's rent.

The $12 in my pocket doesn't do much, but it's something.

I open the front door and hug the volunteer running the circulation desk, dropping the cash in a lockbox. With a green sharpie in hand, I skate over to our donation poster and color in a tiny line to indicate how much closer the new funds bring us to our total goal of $3,500. Scooting back to see the big picture, it's . . . daunting.

My feet ache in my skates so I unlace them and wiggle my toes on the carpet. Despite the dusting of snow, it's warmer in town than up Mount Winter Bliss, so I'm a little sweaty. I head behind the desk and tear off my green puffer. My leg warmers got wet, so I take those off too. Even with my PG-rated strip show, I'm fully clothed in a long thermal top and thick leggings.

Finger combing my hair, I'm sure I look like a mess. I feel like a mess. Let's be real; I am the photo next to the dictionary definition of "mess."

Heading to the front window, I look out, curious if the Johnsons got the banner over the street up. Instead, I see the demon stranger from the corner store. He throws a single suitcase into a shiny black SUV belonging to a rental car chain before resting his bum against the hood and pulling out his phone.

I sigh. Drat. Just passing through, as expected.

I let myself look him over. I've always loved a distinctive nose, and his has a charming bump at the bridge. It's not every day this town gets a burly, bespectacled demon wearing perfectly tailored clothes. I mean, he's practically dressed to seduce a librarian. Who can blame me for ogling a bit?

A smirk quirks across the side of his face. My nose is nearly pressed against the glass at this point, taking in every hunky inch — the light in his eyes, the arch of his metal-capped horns etched with delicate, swirling designs, the way his black hair in a long braid drapes artfully over one side of his face, adding a bit of mystery.

And why is he smiling? I wonder. Maybe his girlfriend sent him racy pictures, some big city woman who wears fancy lingerie every day. No, with my luck he's probably married. This guy is just too put together not to have someone helping him with all that sexiness.

"Up to no Goode, Noey?" Arms envelope me from behind, knocking me out of my horny daydream.

I grip the familiar forearms and crane my head back. "Uncle Darren! I wasn't expecting you until tomorrow."

I lean to the side and wave at the supervisor from the local memory care facility. The orc lady also occasionally volunteers for the library, mostly for big events, but she's been stepping up a lot since Uncle Darren moved in, helping to make sure he still gets to be a part of as much of the library's activities as he can. She organizes these small group visits once a week.

The seniors get to pick out new titles to read, wander around and, I hope, feel less like a patient and more like a person for a few hours.

"The director approved us coming twice a week now since the movie theater is getting renovated."

"I'm so glad." I turn fully and give him a warm hug. When he was in charge here, it was always important that the library felt homey.

Thanks to him, we're more like the town living room, with plenty of floor seating, desks with computers, and comfy chairs along the windows, not to mention sitting stools sprinkled among the quiet, shadowed stacks for the more introverted readers.

While Winter Bliss is changing before my very eyes — a swankier theater, smooth roads, and new shops popping up every day — it's heartening that the library is still a place people want to spend time.

"Oh! My doctor told me about a book I want to check out today. Get this, the premise is a guy answers a newspaper ad: *Teacher seeking pupil.* You won't believe what he finds when he shows up."

"A telepathic gorilla?" I ask, knowing he's talking about one of his favorite books.

"Yeah!" His eyes light up. "That's the one. Sounds pretty good. You've read it?"

More like he read it to me. I smile and try to keep the tears at bay. "I think you'll love it."

It's simultaneously horrifying and fascinating to watch the mind of my favorite person twist itself up in a hundred new ways. And somehow, he finds the most interesting paths back home.

"Aww, little Rom. Not so little anymore, huh?" he asks, peering out the window.

"What?" My heart constricts at the name I haven't heard in years.

"You remember Jaromar? Your best friend when you were . . . how old? When did his family move away?" Uncle Darren's brows scrunch, and it's almost painful to see him falter. His jaw tightens. He often falls into angry frustration when his normally detail-oriented mind can't put the pieces together the way he knows they should fit.

"I was fourteen." I squeeze his hand until he's looking at me again and not chasing hazy thought fragments that lead him to dark places. I always want to bring him back to the present. That's all that really matters anymore, but speaking of the past, this once, might help. "Rom left in the middle of ninth grade."

He looks at me with soft eyes and pats my hand. "That was a tough time. You've always been a sentimental sort, Noey."

I avoid tearing up by giving him another big, rocking bear hug. "Sentimental about you, ya old goof."

He chuckles and hugs me before pulling back. "How are we on the returns stack?"

And he's back in librarian mode, but I can tell by the way he's asking me that he knows it's not him in charge anymore. He knows I'm calling the shots, and that's a relief because I don't have to suffer through a power struggle and can set him to a task for a little bit.

"Go check with Rosie at the circulation desk. She'll need help organizing the incoming books into sections." I have a small but mighty group of volunteers and a couple part-timers. They've been a big help lately, taking on more of the 9-5 tasks while I focus on the fundraiser.

He winks. "On it."

By the time I turn back around to look out the front window, the shiny rental car is gone.

There's no way that was Rom. He hasn't been back to Winter Bliss in almost fifteen years. Besides that, as a kid he had a broken horn and the side of his face was scarred up. I'd have noticed.

My uncle's memories just got tangled up. Every time it happens, the ricochet effect on me is different. Sometimes it's a sweet moment that warms my heart. Sometimes it's heartbreaking. This one? Just a little confusing, I guess.

My phone chimes in my pocket.

"$200?!" I squeak. My mind races. Non-residents can get a library card, though I don't like to do that unless I can trust they won't run off with my books. Then again, I need to weed the collection anyway, so if they take off with some, win-win? And if they're staying for two weeks, they may want a second delivery and be just as generous. Judging by the tone of the message, it's a demon, for sure. Straight and to the point with an offer. And if that offer was $200, it means they've got way more to spare as they always underbid.

I glance back at the donation meter. That wouldn't be one paltry little line. That would be a sizable chunk toward the move. My heart races, hope setting off like doves in flight. My thumbs type out a quick response with a link to our digital library card application.

UNKNOWN NUMBER

> Surprise me.

Hmm. That's a strange response. I grab the keys to my moped and my helmet, then tuck a tiny mace in my pocket for good measure. A lady can never be too careful. $200 for a book delivery for someone who doesn't even have preferences seems too good to be true. Maybe this person is an ax murderer. If so, they know the perfect lure, book talk and a donation to the library.

I'm willing to risk it.

My phone chimes.

UNKNOWN NUMBER

> Sorry, that's weird of me and also not helpful.

I smile, watching the dots dance as my new favorite donor types.

UNKNOWN NUMBER

> I like fantasy and historical fiction.
> Mythologically inspired is even better.
> Five books sounds like a good start.

A good start? That sounds like a repeat donor! A book series drifts to the forefront of my mind, but it's a little racy. Okay, more than a little. I have to ask . . .

Adult content or keep it closed door?

UNKNOWN NUMBER

Surprise me.

UNKNOWN NUMBER

This time, I'm not being weird about it.
I'm good either way.

I chuckle. They seem fun. Even more, I know the perfect book series for them. The payment app I link in the flier chimes. Has there ever been a more beautiful sound than a successful fundraiser? My shoulders shimmy as I restrain a squeal of delight.

Funds received! I'm bringing six books.
Prepare to have your socks knocked off.

"Watch out, Rosie," my uncle says from the circulation desk. "Noey's about to be kicking up a storm rushing around the stacks. She's got some recommendations brewing in that little red head of hers."

No matter how time jumbles in his mind, when he knows me, he knows me. There's nothing I love more than giving someone the perfect book recommendation and introducing them to a story that surprises and delights in a way they never saw coming.

I'm a librarian, after all. It's my specialty.

Chapter Three

Rom

17 years ago

"Oh, Jaromar!" Mister Darren, the human librarian, calls out as I skulk to the back, hunting down my favorite reading spot. "I'm reorganizing that room. You can't go in there today. Why don't you sit at the window seat with Noey?"

My head whips around, lips tight to keep my chin from trembling. Sit with *her*?

"Come on, I'll introduce you. She won't bite." He winks. "Too much."

I gulp. He wants me to sit with Noelle. I know her. She's in sixth grade like me, but we go to different schools. Also, like me, she's here every day. I wondered at first if she was hiding out too but turns out her family likes books. The librarian is her uncle.

Lucky. She's been pretty much surrounded by books her whole life.

And even though we're both eleven years old, she's totally different from me.

Sure, she has red hair, and I have red skin, but that's about all we share. First, she's a girl. Second, she's a human. Then, there's the talking. She talks a lot and to everyone. Young, old, fae, shifter, or demon, nobody makes her nervous. Noelle is always flitting around like a firefly. Every person or stray out-of-place book is another leaf to hop to.

As her uncle and I approach, the sun shines around her, making her red hair look like flames. Myths say that demon goddesses had hair of fire. Maybe that's why I always find myself staring at her.

She sits so still in the window with her eyes down. I wonder if she's sleeping. Then her lips move. The lollipop goes from one side of her mouth to the next. That's the other thing about Noelle: she's got a sweet tooth, whereas I prefer salty snacks.

See? Nothing in common. Total opposites. Why would she want to hang out with me? I'd rather hide out. Do my own thing.

A few weeks ago, when the semester started, I struck the jackpot. My after-school program got canceled, so I've been able to sneak into the library every day right after the bell rings. I have to remember to pry myself away with enough time to make it home for dinner though. My parents don't know, and they're not gonna know if I'm careful. They wouldn't approve of me being here. I haven't lied to them exactly. They just never asked.

And keeping this one tiny secret is the best thing to ever happen to me.

Every day after school, I have three hours to read whatever I want. I already know what my parents would say about my choices. *Fiction, Jaromar? Focus on your practicals. Get your horns out of those adventure books.* They have one dream in life: make a name for our family in the business world. They've struggled their whole lives to make it true. One small business after another fails, and now the pressure is on us, the kids, to succeed where they haven't. All their extra money goes to putting us in the private demon school in town, focused solely on business training. *None of that arts and crafts nonsense*, my dad says.

"Noey, Jaromar needs a place to sit." The librarian taps her on the shoulder. "Will you keep him company?"

She looks up from her book, blinking a few times at her uncle before turning her hazelnut eyes on me. Then she smiles. My face can't help but respond. I smile back but when I feel the tug on my scar, I look away.

"Sit, sit." She grabs my hand and pulls me forward so fast I almost trip. "It's so comfortable here. My favorite spot that nobody knows about because it's back in the maps section and maps are boring, I guess. Oh, that's a shiny cover you've got. It must be new. What're you reading? I've probably read it. I can tell you about all my favorite books."

"Noey." Mister Darren tips his head forward. I'd guess he's annoyed, but his eyes are smiling. "Don't talk his ear off now."

Her lips tuck in on themselves and she makes a zipping motion, settling back onto her side of the window seat.

He looks at me and nods. "Let's keep it quiet, kids."

I nod several times. Fine by me. I have a hard time talking to anyone thanks to this terrible stutter. My *Negotiation Framework* and *Daily Debate* periods are torture at school. The doctors say it's a brain injury but should get better over time.

A few months ago, my brothers and I wandered too far up the mountain, and I fell off a cliff. No joke. One wrong step and now I have a long, ugly gash down the side of my face, scars everywhere, a broken horn, and only half an ear. I was pretty messed up for a while. Still am, I guess. But the week I spent in the hospital also kind of changed my life. The nurses brought me books. They weren't like the ones from school, though. These stories had kids going on all kinds of crazy quests, battling monsters and saving the world. Kids who made friends with all sorts of people.

I peek at Noelle once more before pulling my legs up to lay the book in the crook of my knees.

No matter how many times I try to read the story, I keep going over the same line again and again. It's awkward that she's sitting right next to me, so I glance over my cover. If she's reading too, and I'm just being weird then—

Noelle's staring at me with big eyes. She leans closer and looks to the side, where her uncle just left, then back at me with a whisper. "What're you reading?"

I swallow and lift the book so she can see the spine.

"Eep!" She peeps. I almost laugh because she sounds just like my scarlet finch, Sirocco. "I read that one last week. I won't give it away. I won't. Unless you like spoilers, then I could—"

I shake my head.

"Right. Okay. Don't mind me. I'll be quiet."

She bites her lip and settles back. She's holding a smaller book. The cover is all blue with artwork of a horse running out of the waves.

"Th-that one's s-s-sad," I say, little more than a whisper, then cover my mouth. First words out of my mouth, and I'm spoiling the ending.

"It is," she sighs. "It hurts my heart. But in the end, he gets to live in the ocean where he really belongs. It's a good kind of hurt, don't you think?"

I guess that's true, but I don't make any more words out, just shrug and push my glasses further up my nose. When I get back to reading, my mind finally focuses, and the pages fly by.

Three hours later, my watch chimes. Time to go. I get up and grab my school bag.

"Where are you now?" she asks.

I look at the spot I stuck a scrap of paper in to mark my place. "P-page 113."

She laughs. "No, silly. In the story, where are you?"

"Oh. His grandma's kitchen. She's showing him how to make p-p-p-pasta."

"Ahhh, you'll have fun in the next chapter." Her eyebrows waggle and it makes me laugh.

I nod and start to walk away.

"Bye, Jaromar."

I look back and hug my book tighter, knowing I'll have to shelve it before I leave, that I won't see it, or her, until tomorrow. "It's Rom. You can c-call me Rom."

"Bye, Rom." Her fingers wiggle, then her nose turns back into her book.

"Bye, Noelle."

Present Day

*T*ime to set the stage.

I clap my hands. Sparks fly from my fingertips. *Okay, cool it, Rom. We're not trying to burn down the cabin.*

Nervous energy tends to make my fire powers go a little haywire, and I've got nerves to spare right now.

Noelle is on the way, and I might puke.

I know just what I need to distract myself from real life.

Books.

I grab an armload of them from my carry-on and head to the kitchen, dropping the stack on the coffee table along the way.

Old Ethel's cabin is way nicer than I'd imagined. Mount Winter Bliss isn't known for high quality real estate. The jagged slopes are filled with mostly ramshackle hunting cabins, but she's made something really cozy here. Her property sits on the edge of a cliff, and the back deck has an incredible view of Teapot Lake and the much nicer BZB mountain on the other side of the valley.

The inside is a little dusty, but there are fresh linens in the hall closet and everything is tidy. It's a one-bedroom place with an open concept living and dining area connected to a sunroom along one entire side wall. With all the plants spilling out of the bright room, it feels half cabin, half greenhouse. Judging by how verdant and lush the space is, the elder demoness must come up here often to tend to them.

The greenery is just what I need. I pluck a couple of roses, mindful of the thorns, as well as a few sprigs of some other nice-smelling herbs and place them on the coffee table.

Those will work great.

I unpack my suitcase and place the clothes in the top drawer of a dresser. The next one down has lots of lingerie, brand new with tags on. Oh no. Imagining Old Ethel in that is not something I had on my bingo card for today.

"Sharks in the deep sea. Trash collection. Typos in a great book," I whisper unpleasant things as I shut that drawer, willing the image to vanish. The next one down has candles. *Score!* I finish unpacking and drop the candles alongside the books.

Now, it's teatime. I find a kettle and place it on the gas range. Clicking my fingers, the burner flames to life. I do the same to two of the candles, placing them next to each other on a rough wooden side table.

Perfect.

Waiting for the water to boil, my mind wanders. I check my text messages. Still nothing. Double check the signal strength. One bar. Eugh. I tug on the braid over my shoulder and tell myself to stop being so nervous. Noelle is on her way.

She shouldn't be texting while driving anyway. And the road up was pretty steep, more dangerous than I remember as a kid. What if she got hurt? She's a local, I remind myself. If you're gonna freak out, at least freak out productively.

Right. Pushups. I drop and count out forty reps before the kettle whistles. Rooting around the cupboards, I find a few delicate teacups on the top shelf. Herbal tea, I think. I don't need any more jitters. While concocting the perfect, steamy beverage, I take a short video for the 'gram.

Before drinking it, there's still work to do.

I set the teacup on a saucer, diagonal to the candles, then tug a couple of cloth napkins off to one corner and place some herbs there. Aesthetics are key. I set one of my special edition "Monster Myth Makers" in the center of the spread. It's a limited anthology making waves in the bookish community, and I was able to snag the variant with gold edges. Well, two. This is my reading copy. I keep a collector's copy in my glass-paned bookcase at home.

The final touch, as always, is my bookmark. I slide it from my front pocket into the book so only about an inch of the tattered woven edge pokes out. I may own rare books worth thousands of dollars on the resale market, but my most prized possession is this bookmark I was gifted years ago.

I open my phone and pull up the camera, starting a video. *And . . . Action.*

My fingers snap. Flames dance to life in the viewfinder. I film for six seconds. Anything more doesn't get the same traction on social media. Reviewing the clip, the orange-yellow glow matches the color of the candle and napkins, giving the overall video an artful presentation. With a few quick swipes of a filter and an audio for the video version, I schedule the posts to go up across two social media sites. Hopefully, I can get some internet.

BeastlyandBookish: *Enjoying some downtime with this beefy anthology and a cup of herbal tea. QOTD: What's your drink of choice?*

I switch up the decor on the table and take snaps and videos of three more books, enough content for the coming two weeks. I like to mix up the flat lays with simpler photos of me holding the book against a blurry background. The picture window and sunroom have awesome natural light and prove for great backdrops. I keep my real identity anonymous online, but I show off my hands every few posts. For whatever reason, those get a lot more engagement.

BeastlyandBookish followers continue to grow. It's fun for me to share my love of reading and book collecting, but the biggest benefit is finding new online friends I can geek out with.

I haven't had any friends like that since, well, since Noelle. I glance at the picture window and my heart twists, reminding me of years ago. The first day we met.

To keep myself busy, I drink my tea and rearrange the books on the side table. I packed nine stories off my to-be-read list. I'll be here for two weeks after all. Nine books was just me being realistic about my time. If anything, I underpacked. But I also brought my e-reader. Obviously. I may be a man of leisure when it comes to paid work, but when it comes to reading? I'm no slouch.

I leave the books where they are and straighten my tie. Sweat beads on my forehead between my horns. Get it together, dude. Sure, this girl was my first crush, but she was also my best friend. It's wild to imagine reconnecting with her now. The day my parents pulled me out of school early was heartbreaking. Without warning, we moved away and never came back.

I didn't get the chance to say goodbye.

I step up to the mirror near the front door and straighten my tie before deciding to take it off altogether. *This isn't a freaking business negotiation, doofus.* The sweater is already long gone, and I want to look casual, so I roll up my sleeves and undo the top couple buttons. *Okay, that's better.* It's completely normal to find out that your childhood best friend still lives in your old hometown and that she's grown into a stunning beauty who doesn't wear a wedding ring.

This is fine.

Knock, knock.

"Hello." Her voice is singsong and hits me straight in the chest.

Don't blow it, Rom. I glance back in the mirror and pull my hair to the right, arranging it to cover my scars. The horn!

Shit. I grab the gold-colored caps I like to wear to cover my broken right horn and tug them back on. Okay, that works.

Knock. "Hello?" Noelle says, a little louder.

I open the door and step to the side, waving her in.

She's in skintight leggings and a long sleeve purple top with her coat over her arm, showing off even more of her curvaceous figure than before. I force myself to close my mouth before I start drooling.

"Oh." Noelle says. Her mouth forms a perfect little circle and stays stuck like that. I know she's not the same girl from when I was a kid, but her eyes are, right down to the way she blinks super-fast when she's surprised. "It's . . . it's you."

Chapter Four
Noelle

16 years ago

"Who are you today?"

"A-a-a thief," Rom says, peeking up from his book.

"Jaromar Elond Perchaz." I gasp in mock outrage.

His stutter has gotten better in the last year. He goes to speech therapy, and it's been over a year since the accident. His scars have mostly healed too, going from dark to light pink, but his hair is always hanging down in his face, so I don't see them that often.

"A thief for a good cause." A smile tugs up the left side of his face. "She-She's stealing from the evil empire."

"Hmmph." I grab the book from him and flip through. It has pretty chapter headings. I need to check this one out when he leaves today. It's always fun to read the book he's reading after he leaves and chat about it together the next day. "We'll see."

I pick up the book I was reading. Since I'm trying to grow my hair out, it's a how-to on braiding. I balance the book on my legs and tip my head to the side, grabbing my hair at the temple to separate it into three sections. Thirty seconds of fumbling later, I realize it's not gonna happen. My hair just isn't long enough yet.

I sigh, and Rom glances up from where he was quietly reading beside me. His hair is super long! And I could actually see what I'm doing.

"Hey, can I braid your hair?" I poke his leg.

"Uhhh." Dark, silky strands fall in front of his face. He jerks his head to the side, and it swishes in a long drape, creating a perfectly straight side part.

"Unfair." I pout.

"Huh?"

"Why does a boy get such pretty, shiny hair when he does nothing with it? And I have to live with this frizzy, tangled mess?"

"Your hair is nice," he whispers.

"Your hair is wayyyyy nicer, jerk." I giggle and push his shoulder. "So anyway, can I braid it?"

He shrugs but turns his body on the window bench so his back is to me and starts reading again. We were the same height last year, but he's taller now. Ever since Aunt

Flo started visiting me monthly, the doctor told my mom I won't get much taller.

Again, unfair. Such is a girl's lot in life, I guess.

I page through my book while finger-combing his hair. A classic French braid seems simple enough.

Well, getting around a demon's big, looping horns is not. At all. After five minutes with my fingers in knots, I give up and forget the French part, just focusing on the basic three-strand technique. Okay, that's not so bad. I braid, undo, and re-do it three times before I'm happy with the final product, taking the tie out of my hair to use on his.

I stand up and pull his shoulders around, inspecting my work from the front and sides. He fidgets, glancing up at me then down again.

"You have such nice hair." I pull the long plait over his right shoulder. "I'm jealous."

Rom looks at his feet, but I see the hidden smile. His eyelashes flutter, also way darker and longer than mine. Unfair! His hair is so silky, even that small movement has the strands coming loose at the top. I need to keep practicing, clearly, and maybe try a Dutch braid instead of a French braid next time.

A few strands fall over his right eye, so I push them back behind his torn ear, seeing the healing skin and the scars up close for the first time in a while.

"Do they still hurt?" I ask, wanting to trace the longest of the lines. It's pretty, in a way.

He coughs and pulls back, rearranging the hair at the top to cover his ear, patting it down. "No, n-not anymore."

"Oh. Well, good. And the braid looks nice on you." I cock my head to the side and lean down, not letting up until he looks at me. "You should wear it like that more often."

He smiles, a little crooked and to the left. "Thanks."

Present Day

"Oh. It's you," I say to the demon from the corner store I was thinking about all day.

"It's me," he says on a quiet exhale.

I can barely see half of his face, hidden under the shadow of his hair, but there's a scar marring his upper lip that looks *so* familiar. I study him, rubbing my own lips together, a little chapped from the drive up on my moped. The wind nearly knocked me over on one stretch. They don't call it Last Hour Road for nothing, but I've made the trek before and knew how to manage myself.

Ding. My phone chimes. Service is terrible on this mountain. We're close to the top, so it's a little better up here.

I look down and click on it, reading the first few lines of his library card application.

Wait, seriously?

My eyes blink several times, unbelieving. Still stunned, I catalog this guy's clothing and face, trying to match the large demon before me with the skinny kid I used to know. He wears fancy metal covers over the horn I remember being broken, and his hair must hide the scars I would have recognized right away.

His eyes are the same, though, a piercing red-orange hazel. And a long braid hangs over his right shoulder with the same silky black hair.

"It's you."

I fly at him, banding my arms tight around his middle, noting that my fingertips barely reach across how wide he is.

"Rom, it's really you!"

He exhales and softens, strong arms hugging me back. His palms coast up and down my back, and gosh, it feels so good. So right. I inhale his clean, piney scent and stop myself from rubbing my cheek against his chest like a cat.

"Oh geez!" I pull back, suddenly realizing just because I remember him doesn't mean he remembers me. "I'm sorry. Do you even . . .? It's Noelle. Do you remember? I don't make a habit of tackling every new person I meet, but we knew each other as kids. You stopped by the library every day, and we used to be friends and—"

"Best friends," he says while angling his face slightly away, though his gaze drifts back. "I remember. Hi, Noelle."

I smile and lean toward the side of his face he's hiding, trying to put him at ease. I never cared about his scars. Why would he hide from me? Well, I guess it has been a while.

"It's so good to see you again. I didn't recognize you at first. You're very, ahem, different," I say, clearing my throat. He looks nervous. *Okay, stop ogling him, geez. Be cool.* "How are you? What've you been up to? How is your family?"

Where did you go? I purse my lips together and grab my strawberry lip gloss to put on, an emergency attempt to shut the heck up. *Was your new town bigger than Winter Bliss? Better?* Questions ping through my mind, but I manage to hold them in. *Why didn't you find a way to contact me? Why didn't I?*

Did you miss me?

"Fine. I'm g-good." He fidgets with the end of his braid, barely making eye contact. "Live in Austin, just working and keeping my head down. Family's alright. We see each other all the time, too much probably, seeing as how we work together." He chuckles and when we make eye contact again, he stops talking, just blinks at me like he can't believe it's me.

Well, buddy, the feeling is mutual.

"That's great," I say, nearly breathless. I can't believe he's really here. My mind is a beehive of conflicting thoughts, unable to place the burly man before me with the boy I used to know. His shyness seems the same, as charming as ever, making me just want to hug and reassure him at every turn. His eyes dart around the room, determined not to look at me. I cringe, realizing I made him nervous somehow. I probably pried too much, overloaded him with a bunch of questions, then didn't pick up the conversation because I was lost in my own head.

I'm too much sometimes, and I know it. *Okay, Noelle. Stick to the script. You're a librarian on a book delivery.* I change the subject to safer topics. Books.

"Well, consider your library card application accepted." I put out my hand.

He shakes it with an amused half-smile, and my heart pitter-patters at the contact. *Oh dear heavens*, his grip is solid. His hands are huge and veiny. My gaze travels slowly up his hairy forearms to his chest, then his face. And he's staring at me. And we're both saying nothing again.

I wiggle out of his grasp and straighten. "Your text mentioned that you're in town for a couple weeks?"

"Yep." He runs a hand over his horn cap and backs up against a side table, knocking something over that makes several thudding sounds.

They looked like books. "Are those . . ."

"Nothing. I'll pick it up later." He leans against the wall, blocking my view of whatever fell. "I'm a big reader, so I'll probably keep you busy with book requests."

I grin and step further into the cabin. "I brought six."

"Child's play." He smirks and gestures me toward the couch. "I'll be done with those quick enough."

My eyebrows lift, amused. He was a speed reader as a kid too, took some kind of class at his school. I guess the habit stuck.

"If I even click with them." He shrugs.

"Oh ho ho," I crow. Now that's a challenge I always win. "You will! At least one of the two trilogies." I lob my bag onto the couch and bring out the first book, handing it to him.

As he looks over the cover, doubt colors his face. I get it, considering it's a half-naked lady. He pulls out the laminated paper I stuck in the middle.

"The Least Deadly Hikes of Mount Winter Bliss?" he reads the title and gives me a curious look.

"Your text made it seem like you were new to town, but the address was so high up, I figured if you wanted to go hiking, it's good to be informed. I have a few of those trifolds at the library. Better safe than sorry, you know?"

"I'm not much of a hiker." He gestures at the scarred half of his face. "After all this."

"Oh." That's right. The accident from when he was younger. I think the memory of him so injured as a kid is partly why I stock these maps in the library. "Oh no, I'm so sorry." Gosh, I feel horrible. Not that I knew *he* was the person in the cabin, but still.

"It's okay. Really thoughtful, actually. I'm sure a future guest will appreciate it." He chuckles while setting the map to the side and waggles the book at me. "I'm more of a stay-inside-and-read-about-cool-heroes-who-hike kind of guy. Tell me about these."

"Well, good news. They do hike!" I brighten. "So here's the premise. It's a fantasy world where only humans exist."

"Pfft. Boring," he says. "Humans love fantasies where they're the only ones left alive on the earth."

Well, he's not wrong about that. Kinda depressing if you ask me. He turns the book over to read the summary on the back before peering up at me. I square my shoulders and take a deep breath, readying my monologue.

"Okay so . . ." I chop the air in front of us, using my hands to help illustrate the selling points. "The world is separated into the worship of a bunch of immortal beings who believe in different ways of expressing love. They're humans but not like regular humans. The heroine is this magical pain slut chosen by her god to save the world. And her travel companion is this super celibate monk warrior. As you might have guessed, sparks fly, and sexy hijinks ensue."

His eyes bug out of his head. Okay, maybe I sensationalized it with the magical pain slut bit.

"It sounds like a lot, but it's really cool," I say. Undeterred, I shake my head and bring out a different book. "And in case that doesn't float your boat, I brought the second trilogy in the series. Same world, but a couple decades later. The hero is a younger guy in line for the throne, but his mother was an evil villain, and he worries he'll become one too someday." I smile brightly and waggle my eyebrows. "Less sado-masochistic sex scenes, if that's a plus or a minus."

Probably more his speed. He picks up the second book but keeps peeking at the first. I think I hooked him.

"Thanks. They sound like a wild ride." He takes the stack of six and sets them on the kitchen table. "Though I'm surprised I haven't heard about them on bookstagram."

"Bookstagram?" My nose scrunches. "Is that like candy grams for books? A messenger does a little song and dance to sell you on a story's premise? Hold on! That's a great idea to spice up the fundraiser." I pull up my phone and whisper a voice memo. My voice isn't half bad. I bet people will find that charming.

He chuckles and pulls up his phone, turning it to me. "No, it's a hashtag on Nymphstagram that readers and book lovers use to share their reviews, home libraries, and special editions."

He scrolls through dozens of brightly colored images.

"Oh my goodness, that's pretty."

There are book covers with shiny foil, fairy lights in reading nooks, and barely dressed readers wearing lingerie. Whoa. Stacks and stacks of books in pretty rooms with bouquets and coffee. So much coffee.

"A book lying on a bunch of flowers. I never imagined reading could look so . . . magical."

I make a mental note to try that. Photos can't be too hard, right? I should really figure out social media one of these days.

"Yeah. It's pretty neat." He clicks on something else and pulls up a new page showing a well-coordinated set of photos all in a warm tones. "This is my account."

I read the profile name and snort, glancing at him sideways. "BeastlyandBookish?"

"I love books, and I mean . . ." He gestures in a circle around his face.

"Ex-squeeze me?!" I wave a dramatic circle around my own face, horrified by what I think he's implying. "What is that supposed to mean?"

"You have eyes, Noelle." His jaw tightens, then slides back and forth, something he used to do when he was upset, usually at himself. "While I'm sure everybody in town including me had a crush on you, I've always looked like this."

"You're far from beastly!" I scoff, offended on his behalf. He had a crush on me back then? I swallow, my heart racing, replaying our friendship from years ago and where I missed that.

"Thank you for saying that." He angles his head away and finger-combs hair over the right side of his face. "I've got an ugly mug. It's fine. Facts are facts." He sighs and pats his belly. "And I've kind of let myself go."

I glare at him. There are few things that get me more riled up than people talking down on themselves. The world does enough of that to us already. Not to mention, it's always lies!

"Jaromar Elond Perchaz," I poke his chest to the beat of each name and push closer. "You are the gentle giant! The smart kid with glasses! The magic spark character that makes a book worth reading!"

He gulps, cheeks darkening all the way up to his horns. "You think so?"

"I know so! Ugly? Let yourself go? Ugh. That's the kind of talk that sets everyone back. I mean, big guys are all the rage right now. Plenty of folks would love to climb you like a tree!"

As soon as I say it, I can't help but imagine myself doing just that and my body flushes, head to toe. I can feel the warmth, a discoloring combination of embarrassment and arousal, the redhead's bane.

"Oh, yeah?" His smile seems surprised.

"Yeah!" I'm really on fire now, in more ways than one, pushing my palms against his broad chest like I'm trying to pick a fight with him, even though he doesn't budge an inch. I just seem to be getting closer and closer, and my goodness he's warm. "I won't have you talk about yourself like that!"

"Or what?" he asks, voice darker. Intimate.

"Or I'll . . . I'll . . . I'll show you!"

And I kiss him. I grab two fistfuls of his white shirt and yank him down to my mouth.

Oh.

He kisses me back, mouth hungry and entreating, as he grabs my face, the pads of his fingers tracing my jaw, then the back of his knuckles down my neck.

Oh, that's nice.

I sigh, sparks of pleasure flickering to life inside me. The kiss slows from its first frantic instincts and grows leisurely, even better somehow. His body, so big and wide, fits against me perfectly. He holds me so tenderly, pulling me closer. Demons run hot, I know this on a scientific level, but I really *feel* it now for the first time. How cozy and safe it is to be held by him. Each warm exhale is like a drug, dragging me deeper into this weightless haze.

When my hand finds his cheek, I feel the scar. The big one he's always hiding. It's a long branching mark that pulls at the corner of his lip and puckers the skin in a couple of places.

He pulls back, watching me carefully. This close, I really see him, the boy I used to know. The dark eyes, roiling red and orange like demons do when their emotions run hot. The same nose, crooked and off center, just a little bigger these days. Everything about him is bigger. His face turns to the side, and my hand slips free.

"So, anyway." I touch my cheek, feeling flushed. My face must be a sight, no doubt red as a tomato. "There you have it."

I made my point that he's not ugly by attacking him with my mouth. *Great job, Noelle. That should do it.* It seemed an effective strategy until he pulled back when I touched his scars.

Rom's gaze on me is curious though, not upset. "Is it okay if I text you my thoughts on the books?"

"Of course." I exhale with relief. He's polite enough not to tease me or make this into a super awkward thing. I smooth my hair, gone a little loose with the make out, and tuck some errant strands behind my ear. "I reread them just a couple months ago. It's one of my favorite series."

"Great."

"Cool."

"Awesome."

Okay, that's quite enough dilly-dallying. I clear my throat and straighten my posture. Back in librarian mode. "They're due back in a week. I can drive back up here to—"

"No need," he interrupts. "I'll be done sooner than that. Can I drop them off at the library? I'd love to see the place again."

"Oh, okay, sure." A pang squeezes my heart because I know we'll have to move soon, and he seems so eager to see the building we spent every afternoon in as kids. I pick up my mostly empty bag and throw it over my shoulder. "We're open daily from 10 to 7. What are you, um. . ." My curiosity is getting the better of me now that I can think straight. "Why are you in town?"

"I'm opening a coffee shop." He straightens and fists his hands at his hips, transformed into a more confident version of himself, the guy I noticed in the corner store, the one I thought was a stranger. "It's the family business. Our chain of stores is called *Perkatory*."

"That's so clever." I beam, catching the triple play on words. "Good for you guys. And good for Winter Bliss. We could use a coffee shop. Miss Ethel's drip isn't cutting it."

With an easy laugh, he follows me to the door, holding it open as I trek down the snowy steps.

"Yeah, and the library is right next door to our new location," he says.

Time slows. That can't be right. There's only one building adjoining the library, and I'm going to rent it. My mind races as he leans against the doorjamb, looking so happy and at ease.

"Where is it?" My voice comes out with a squeak. I must have misheard. "Right . . . right next to the library?"

"The old antique store that's been sitting empty. Big windows in the front."

I shake my head. My stomach drops to my toes, and everything goes numb.

"Hey, are you . . ." He steps forward. "Are you okay?"

"Yes."

Oh no, no, no. What can I do? What can't I do? Is there anything that can save the library when the only feasible rental in town just went up in smoke?

"I've gotta go."

"I've gotta go."

Chapter Five
Rom

15 years ago

"You're the best." Noelle plucks the lollipop out of my hand, unwraps it, and plops it straight in her mouth. I get her candy from the corner store pretty much every day.

"No prob." I shrug. Even though I don't love sweets that much, she does, and it kinda makes the air smell nice when we read together. Is that weird? Probably.

"I made you something." Noelle's hands are cupped closed. The lollipop moves from one side of her mouth to the other.

If this was one of my brothers, I'd already be prepping to fight because it'd definitely be a stinky beetle or poisonous toad or something horrible. But Noelle is too nice for that.

When her fingers unfurl, a multi-colored strip of handwoven threads lays across her palm.

I'm . . . confused.

"It's a friendship bracelet." She seems a little nervous at my stunned reaction. "Sort of. I mean, it *is* a friendship bracelet, but I made it a little bigger because I didn't really know if you'd want a bracelet. I figured I'd make you something different, because *we're* kind of different, you know?" She's rambling. Her hands take up the motion, rolling and poking at the air as she talks. "So anyway, I was reading this new craft book, and it came with these supplies already part of the whole book set thingy, and I saw this really cool design and was like — Rom needs this! It took a while, and I kind of flubbed part of it, but I think it's—"

"It's awesome." I grab one end and feel the texture beneath my fingers, so soft. I can't believe I was the first person she thought to make a friendship bracelet for, even if it's not a bracelet, I guess. "Thank you."

The woven craft is about the length of my outstretched palm and fingers and a couple inches wide. Too big for a bracelet, sure. The design is an intricate pattern of gray, white, and blue. There's a blocky "R" on one end and an "N" on the other. White blobs stitched in the middle draw my attention — shapes that seem to connect the two letters. It almost looks like . . .

"Are these hearts?" I ask. My pulse races. **N <3 <3 <3 R**. Does she *like me,* like me? I know I like her a lot, but we're friends, and I've been too afraid to say—

"What? No!" She chuckles and leans in to look closer at her design as if it's crazy I said that. I turn away, embarrassed. Of course. I'm ugly. Besides the scars, I barely have an ear on one side, and my nose doesn't line up right anymore. I definitely don't look anything like the few demon boys who have girlfriends at thirteen.

Noelle is just creative and super thoughtful. Clearly, she didn't mean it like that. I bet all the guys at her school have a crush on her too.

She traces the white shapes, looking at the design closer. "These are the snowy tops of the mountains, like Mount Winter Bliss and the BZB." She turns her head this way and that. "It does kind of look like hearts though. My art teacher would call that a *beautiful oops.*"

I brush my thumb over the "N" end of the braided item, still feeling kind of dumb. She holds the other side and slides her thumb over the "R."

A friendship bracelet. Or something.

Leaning forward, she grasps my pinky finger with hers. Bright brown eyes meet mine. Her red hair is so pretty and wild when little pieces come out of her ponytail.

"Best friends forever?" she asks.

I take a breath. Everything is alright. We're cool. Just because I have a crush on her doesn't mean it has to be weird.

I nod. "Best friends forever."

When she smiles again, I do too. It's impossible not to. She drops the handmade gift in my palm, and I trace the long design again, seeing what she was going for. It looks like home. A mountain range. Snow and big skies. An "R" for Rom and an "N" for Noelle.

"If it's not a bracelet, what is it?" I loop the whole thing over and over around a finger, then unloop and repeat. I decide it's definitely the nicest gift I've ever gotten.

"Something you'll use more." She grabs the book from my lap and flips to where I marked my place with a ripped off page of my school notebook. She tosses it to the side and holds the book back out to me, fully open.

I lay it in the crease between the pages. "A bookmark?"

"A *friendship* bookmark." She waggles her eyebrows. "This way, if someone takes your book after you leave, they'll see it and know it belongs to someone, then turn it in to lost and found. But I'll be here, and I'll let them know the book is already checked out to my best friend who's coming back tomorrow, and they'll just have to find something else to read."

My chest feels tight. "That's smart."

Noelle's just nice like that, thinking of others, often in ways that don't make any kind of sense to me. But in her own way, she's trying to help everybody all the time. I don't tell her that I hide my book behind the dustiest stack of

Farmer's Almanacs in the Rare Books section. No one ever finds my treasures.

"It's the best friend code," she says. "We look out for each other."

I nod. "We do."

Present Day

She's avoiding me.

I mean, Noelle is the soul of politeness, always has been, even when we were kids.

But the kiss.

No. I shake my head. *Get a grip. She regretted it.* I mean, she left in a flurry of motion and excuses. Before I could catch my breath, her moped was careening down Last Hour Road.

I glance at myself in the hall mirror, a mess of jagged scars and half-torn ear and crooked nose.

It was a pity kiss. You were talking down on yourself. Noelle was always too nice for her own good. I grit my teeth and try to see it from her perspective. It doesn't have to mean anything. I can play it cool.

So, I dive into the books. The first in the series has smooth worn edges and a few pages in the middle nearly falling out, but damn it smells good. A nostalgic mustiness combined with ink and a light floral note that must be the library. No, the scent of Noelle. She mentioned rereading it recently, and it was probably this exact copy.

I lay on the couch for a moment with the book across my face, just breathing it in like a lovesick dolt. *Pathetic.* I shake some sense into myself and start reading.

Four hours later, I'm slack jawed. This book is kind of insane — high fantasy with a unique twist. The political intrigue and upended power dynamics are so gripping, I can barely tear myself out of my seat even though my stomach has been growling for the past half hour.

Noelle knows her books. She may not be aware of the current buzziest books on social media, but hot damn the woman has taste. And this particular storyline sets off a million questions in my mind. What does she like about it? The intimate scenes are intense, to say the least. Should I be taking notes or is her interest purely in the plot? Does she swoon for male romantic interests like this guy — stoic and duty bound?

I stand up to make some dinner and straighten my clothes. I connect with the character in some ways, but how would I be described if I were a hero in a story?

The magic spark character. Pfft. No way.

But she kissed me.

I kissed my childhood crush! It doesn't feel real. For the umpteenth time since she left, I rub my lips together. The taste of her fruity gloss still lingers, and it's the sweetest kind of torture. I want more of her, however I can get it.

As I continue reading, I text her my reactions to the first book. When she finally responds hours later, it's a thumbs up emoji. Oof. I'm no expert in flirting by any stretch of the imagination, but a thumbs up emoji?

That's as platonic as you can get.

Rather than blowing up her phone, I lose myself in reading. Before I know it, I'm closing the cover on book six and three days have just flown by. I'm a little disoriented, and my body feels kind of stiff from disuse.

A solo vacation to a cabin in the woods sounds nice in theory, nothing but me and my books and the silence of nature, but by the end of day three, I find myself making my evening tea and realize I haven't uttered a word since Noelle left.

I like my alone time, but an illogical thought pops into my head. Can someone lose their voice if they stop using it? I emit a noise just to reassure myself, and it comes out as a sad, hoarse croak.

Yikes. Hermit time is over. I need to get back into town.

For practical reasons, of course — groceries, more firewood, and a strong enough Wi-Fi to upload the social media posts for my bookish accounts. If it's also an excuse to stop by for another personalized recommendation from my favorite librarian, I mean, who can blame me?

I head into town. It's a couple days before the big human gift-giving holiday, Christmas, and storefronts have window displays and last-minute sales running. People rush from store to store with gifts. The excitement for the holidays is electric. I know from here on out, the town will be bustling until the big festival on New Year's Eve, advertised by a massive banner with a charming fire and ice theme that hangs across Main Street.

Man, it's good to be back in my childhood hometown, but why on Earth is everything so small? It almost looks like a fake Western town version of the places I used to know. The buildings are so tiny and look older than I remember. Two grown people can barely fit on a sidewalk we used to walk three across as kids.

This place is familiar but different. I guess that's the price of growing up.

And the price of parking? Astronomical. I pull my car into a lot advertising an hourly rate that's equal to a healthy kidney on the black market.

The weathered orc running the lot is a tough negotiator, but I'm tougher, growling and flashing the scarred side of my face. One thing I learned as I got older is how to use my fearsome looks to my advantage. It mostly pays off in intimidating these kinds of guys or during tough business deals, not so much with romantic prospects. Once I get a spot, I sit in my car for a few minutes because the cell signal is strong enough to finally catch up on social media. I upload my posts, check on a few of my friends, and get a sense for the newest book taking the community by storm.

But I can only doom scroll for so long. It's time. I'm going to ask Noelle out for coffee. Shoot, there's no coffee shop yet. Uh, brunch? Yeah, I'll ask her to brunch and gauge her response. Maybe she's just not that into me.

I stroll up to the library's stained-glass windows and hype myself up. My hands tremble as I smooth down my hair, re-tie my braid, and straighten my glasses, giving myself an inner pep talk worthy of an inspirational poster.

If she brushes me off, it's okay. I'll survive. I'm just visiting anyway. Rejection will hurt worse in person than being ignored through text, but at least I can put this infatuation behind me.

A sign at the front drop box for books still reads: *If library is open, please return inside.* The sign isn't just a way to avoid damaging the books with repeated drops, but a chance for the staff to ask how we liked a book or what we're looking for next. Small towns are nosy, but it's not always in bad ways.

I open the door. There's no bell chime or announcement of entry. The library is a quiet place, yet somehow always primed for conversation. A straight-back chair sits beside the front desk for chats with staff on duty. I remember as a kid how random people would stop by and chime in with their thoughts. Soon enough, an accidental book club discussion had begun.

Her uncle sits in the old chair today, chatting with two teenage student workers, pointing this way and that. The surly one of the pair, a dark-haired demon girl scoots away, working at the computer and typing in returns. The other, a fae boy with lavender skin and bright green eyes, nods and smiles enthusiastically at Mr. Goode's stories.

I hold my breath as I approach. Will he recognize me?

As I stand behind someone checking out, he glances up. His face is older, hair lighter with stark streaks of silver. He seems shorter too, but I know it's just because I've grown taller. His smile is the same though, which he flashes at me briefly before turning back to the fae boy.

He doesn't know who I am.

I rub my chest, surprised how much it hurts. I shouldn't expect him to remember me on the spot like that, should I? So much has changed. At the same time, he was such an influential person to me as a kid. He knew all my favorite books and how my grades were doing semester by semester.

Now? Nothing. I'm a stranger. Forgettable.

And probably not just to him. Do I really expect to pick up where I left off with Noelle too? Surely, I've been gone too long.

She doesn't date outsiders.

"Is Noelle in?" I ask the young fae.

Her uncle cocks his head at me. "You know Noey?"

"An old friend," I say, too embarrassed to give my name and risk him making a halting apology or worse yet, genuinely having no memory of me.

Mr. Goode nods, but his gaze is a little distant. A friendly-looking orc woman comes up and touches his shoulder, taking away his attention. The way she smiles and watches him so carefully, it almost seems like she's helping him. But he's not elderly enough to need coddling, maybe in his early sixties?

"Sorry, Noelle just left." The fae answers me with a smile, both hands busy crocheting demon horn warmers. Adorable holiday tradition and entirely decorative. Horns don't need warming. "She's had a lot going on with the big fundraiser on New Year's Eve."

Hmm. The fundraiser. That's right. I paid my $200 to get her up to the cabin but didn't really dwell on it. She does sound busy.

"Thanks." I knock on the countertop and head out, still a little unsettled at how Mr. Goode took no notice of me.

After a quick trip to the general store for supplies, I catch a flash of red hair and neon green as I load up my rental car.

Noelle zooms down the sidewalk in her roller skates, doing a little twirl to avoid colliding with a gaggle of kids. She gesticulates and points to the library, looking like a living marshmallow in her puffer jacket, all sweetness and curves.

When she darts into the general store, I follow.

"Rom!" Her hand flies to her chest.

I duck my head, suddenly nervous. Angling the good side of my face her way, I stuff my hands in my pocket. "I finished the series."

"No, you didn't!" Her mouth falls open. "It's only been a couple days."

"You forgot I was a speed reader?" I paste on a confident smirk. Maybe she's forgotten as much about me as her uncle. "They were excellent by the way. I mean, I skimmed the second trilogy if I'm honest, but you can expect a 5-star book report."

"That's great." She smiles, but there's a tightness in her expression as her gaze darts around. "Listen, I gotta grab a bunch of stuff. Storybook circle is starting soon, and I'm so behind."

"I'll help." If she's trying to brush me off, I'll just call it a day and—

"Oh, please." She sighs. "Thank you so much!"

We split the list. I take on the craft supplies while she grabs food. She needs drawing pads, glue, markers, ten different colors of thread, and the list goes on. When she gets to the checkout, I step up and slide my credit card through the payment reader. $225. They really inflate the cost of everything in these small towns. Definitely something I need to factor into Perkatory's menu prices.

"I can't let you pay for all this." Her hand covers mine, and even though demons run hot, she still feels warm to me, like our temperatures are perfectly calibrated.

"Consider it my next donation. I need more books, after all."

"I really owe you a good one then," she says, bagging up everything in a flash. "Man, I'm not sure I can top the last series." The little checkout countertop is so small that as she fills each bag, I try to juggle holding them. By the end, I run out of room in my arms and start looping the bags over my horns, balancing two paper bags on each side of my head.

When she looks up, holding the last bag full of wrapping paper, she doubles over, laughing. "You used to crack me up so hard when you'd do that."

"Happy to serve." I bow lightly and the bags swing, nearly crashing together in front of my face.

She laughs harder, and we make our way back to the library.

"I had a thought about a good story for you last night just as I was falling asleep," she says as she comes back from putting groceries away. "But *FWOOP*, it just shot straight out of my head. If I don't make a note of it, I swear I'd never be able to hold on to a single solitary thought."

Her voice goes a mile a minute. I forgot how fun it is to just listen to her ramble. Her brain twists and turns in the most interesting directions.

"I know I can come up with something, though." she continues. "I'll sit down after this next class and think of a really good one for you. I promise. It's just that I've been so, so, so. . ."

"Busy?" I ask.

"Yeah." She sighs and her posture wilts, like the weight of the entire world is on her shoulders.

Noelle isn't avoiding me. After hearing about everything she's got on her plate, I ditch the plan to ask her for brunch. It feels a little selfish. I'll meet her where she's at and try to help her with whatever she needs. It's what a friend would do.

Chapter Six

Noelle

14 years ago

I wore my favorite Christmas sweater today.

It's pretty cute. A cropped, tight-fitting style in red and green with glittery threads for the lights on the embroidered tree. I snap off some of the unraveled bits and stare out the front stained-glass windows of the library. Rom should be out of school already.

He's late.

Today is the last day before winter break and everyone was supposed to dress up to celebrate our favorite upcoming holiday. Even though my family isn't religious, I've always loved the gift-giving tradition of Christmas. I bet Rom's just wearing his uniform since he goes to a fancy private school.

I almost wore my sunny yellow dress to celebrate The Advent of the Honest. It's a demon winter holiday all about sunlight and the end of the cold, dark days. It's actually my favorite over Christmas. I guess I just felt kind of weird celebrating it. Even though I grew up in a town full of demons, I'm not really one of them.

But who wouldn't love the New Year's Eve celebration? It's so fun! The Truthfire Festival starts with a parade of stilt walkers and oversized puppets. Street vendors sell hot apple cider and kettle corn and any kind of food that can be made over fire. I always help my uncle man the library booth in the market square.

The only thing I've never been to is the midnight party. It's when everyone counts down to the New Year. There are torches and ritual fires, and the demons do this crazy fire-magic thing to make the lava flow on Mount Winter Bliss. It's just the *coolest*. But I've only ever watched the volcano light up from my bedroom window. It's super late at night and an adults-only thing. Boo.

This year, I think I'm gonna sneak in.

I mean, I'm fourteen, which is basically grown up. I bet most people who don't know me wouldn't even bat an eye.

I can't wait to tell Rom! I know he'll go with me since he already sneaks out to the library every day. He's a demon, and he'll know way more about the fire-magic stuff. I want to see it in person so bad but only if Rom goes with me. We've been friends for three years now but have never met up outside the library. Which is why I'm wearing my cutest outfit to ask him. I'll beg and plead and there's no way he'll say no.

So I stand at the front window and wait for him to show up, but he's already thirty minutes late. That's not like him at all. He comes in every day after school at exactly the same time. If anything, he should have gotten an early release like my school.

It sounds crazy, but I'm honestly kind of sad the school semester is over. Most kids would be jumping up and down to have three weeks off, but it's my last day to see Rom for a while. New Year's Eve is right in the middle of winter break though, so if we can plan to sneak out and meet up, it won't be so hard.

I like spending time with him. A lot.

The winter break will be so boring without him. I'll miss his smile and the sound of his voice; how warm it feels to sit next to him in the window because he's always running a little hotter than me. It just . . . feels nice.

A couple days ago, I caught myself doodling hearts in the margins of my book and realized I had a little bit of a problem.

I have a crush on my best friend.

It's been driving me kind of crazy. Should I keep it to myself? I'm so bad at secrets. Should I tell him? I mean, what would he say?

Then I came up with the perfect plan. New Year's Eve. The Truthfire Festival. That's when I'll tell him. It's the Advent of the Honest, after all. Demons believe it's the one night a year you have to tell the truth, the whole truth, and nothing but the truth.

No matter what.

I rub at my forearm. There's still smudged lipstick from the last hour where I practiced kissing my arm. It's kind of embarrassing, but practice makes perfect, you know?

New Year's Eve. I'll tell him I like him and ask him if he likes me too.

I press my nose up against the glass until it fogs.

Still no sign of Rom. I wonder where he went?

Present Day

"I missed this place." Rom looks over the bookcases close by, the tall ceilings, and the spiral staircase in the back.

I missed you being here too, I want to say but bite my lip. It's been over a decade. We were just kids! Do we even know each other anymore? Then, he gives me that same bashful smile he always did, and my cheeks warm in response.

"I don't really know anything about the history of the library." He fists his hands at his hips, making him look even taller, his back even broader. "It seems unusual that it's privately owned and not public, right?"

"Yeah," I chuckle, moving the classroom crafts into one bag and wrapping paper to another. "The library just sort of happened, and no one's really changed much about how we work. It all started over a hundred years ago as a reading room right here." I wave around the tall open space we're in. The first floor is for the circulation desk, large seating area, and computer center with the only shelves along the walls and back section. The center is an open atrium to the second floor where long walkways wrap around all sides with bookcases along each wall. "Originally, this building was an opera house built by some rich demon settler, but it never took off. Something that swanky in Winter Bliss. Can you imagine?"

"I can see it." He smiles, his gaze drifting over the second floor. The upper-level balconies still have the original brass filigree railing. It's a chore to shine, which is why they're a little dull right now.

I point up to the Non-Fiction Autobiographies section. "The second floor is where the higher-priced ticket holders would have looked down on the actors down here."

As if on cue, an elegant older fae over in Periodicals shushes us. Her eyes soften when she sees it's me.

"Sorry, Mrs. Clare." I wave and whisper to Rom. "Noise carries since it's a big open space, so we do have to be a little more *'shhhh'* happy with the chatty patrons."

"Patrons only or does that extend to the staff too?" He's smirking at me, surely remembering how often Uncle Darren told us to pipe down over in the window seat when we were kids. Well, not really *us* so much as *me*.

"Anyway" — I give him a friendly shove — "my family has managed this place ever since that old opera house went belly up, though we've never owned the building. It changes hands every now and again. The current landlord is this big real estate company from out of town. They're nice and all."

Rom looks pensive. "I sense a *but* coming."

I sigh and hop to sit on the counter, tapping the heel of my skates against the wood paneling. "*But* they raised the rent. I mean, rent is rising across town because of all the money flowing in from the resort. Business is booming or whatever. It makes sense. I get it. But my funding is basically . . . well, it's not booming. It's a flat line. Decades ago, my uncle set us up as a nonprofit and got this local petition going to have the town formally contract us as the local library. It's a twenty-year agreement with a set budget, and there's still two years to go."

"Aren't libraries funded on property taxes? I'm sure those are increasing." His brow furrows. "I've done my research, and Winter Bliss is in a bit of an economic boom, as you said."

"I don't really know." I shrug. "I've got to make do until the end of this contract and hope we're serving the public well enough to get renewed."

"Of course you will." He looks almost offended. "This place is amazing."

I grin and puff out my chest. "Thanks. Well, a lot of that is the inter-library partnerships, technology nonprofits, and literacy organizations that help us out. My librarian friends from bigger cities send me their surplus books too. The whole back room is an embarrassment of riches right now."

"Full of books?" His eyes bug out.

I smile. It's nice to see Rom is as book obsessed as he used to be. "Yeah! You wanna see?"

He nods, rubbing his hands together with obvious excitement. I skate to the back room and open the door.

Taking a deep inhale, I turn around. His eyes close slowly on a groan.

"Is there anything better than the smell of old books?" I tease. A lot of them are leather bound too, which is even better.

He shakes his head. "I could kiss you."

I bite my lips together to hide my smile.

He clears his throat and opens his eyes, taking stock of the giant mess and studiously avoiding my gaze. "So, uh, these aren't all organized yet?"

"To say the least. I keep meaning to get around to it." I skate a careful path through stacks of books on the floor, tables, and in various boxes perched precariously on top of each other.

"What about your volunteers and staff?"

"Oh, I hate to make them do all this busywork. I'll get to it, eventually." I lug one box onto a table at the back and crack it open. "It's a mess in here because I had to close down the Rare Books section when I took over last year, so all of those are in here too."

"Why'd you close down Rare Books?" he asks.

Speak of the devil, I pull out one of the oldest ones we have. It's delicate, part of the Farmer's Almanac collection that dates back to our first year as a reading room. They're more for show than use, but it hurts that they aren't in their glass-paned shelves anymore.

"Budget crunch. I couldn't bear to let my student assistants go. They work here part time and during school holidays." My voice catches a little, but I shake my head and focus on the present. "It's an important job for them, good experience for college, you know? So when my apartment lease came up, I closed Rare Books, cut my salary, and moved into that space. It's nice. There was already a full bathroom. I just had to get a little work done to make a kitchen happen." I move the almanac into the *Keep* box and the next two paperbacks into *Give Away*. "They're still back here if we get a request, but no one really visited Rare Books much anyway."

"Your uncle always loved that section," Rom says.

I nod, afraid to speak because I might cry. It wasn't an easy choice. In a way, it felt like burying a piece of him by moving these boxes out of sight, and I hate that. But no matter what I do, there's always a sacrifice. Right now, all I can do is look ahead, do whatever I can to keep the library open. That's what Uncle Darren would want.

"Is he . . . okay?" Rom asks softly.

I shake my head and try to calm the emotion clawing up my throat by finishing out this box and moving onto a stack of donations. Keep pushing forward.

Rom rifles through a box, gingerly touching the spine of some older church records that are probably more than 150 years old.

"It's early onset dementia," I finally manage to say. "He lives in a home down the street. Visits pretty often though."

Rom looks up, surprise and sympathy written across his face. "I'm sorry. I saw him today. He didn't recognize me. I thought—"

I smile. "He actually knew who you were before I did. The other day, you were across the road about to get into your car, and he pointed you out to me. *Little Jaromar*, he said."

"Yeah?" He rubs his chest, then smirks at me. "So he recognized me, but you didn't?"

"You don't look quite the same, my friend." I wave up and down. *Not so little anymore.* "Taller, broader. Plus the horn caps, and I only saw the side of your face that day."

Almost like he does his best to hide away. I think I've embarrassed him because his cheeks darken, and he picks up a book from another box.

"Oh my gosh." I skate over and grab it from him. I'd recognize that yellow dust jacket anywhere.

"Ishmael?" he asks, reading the title.

"It's a first edition, first printing." It's not the one my uncle read all the time. That was a paperback, nearly worn to shreds. This was the copy he got autographed when the author stopped by Winter Bliss on vacation, total fluke.

My palm passes over the book's front, and I can't help it. I slide off the front half of the dust jacket and trace the embossed front of the hardcover. It's not *that* special, but to me, to my uncle, it sure is.

"I have a friend who could help get a value on the books you want to part with." He points to the *Give Away* pile and has his phone up. A digital photo of Ishmael is in a little square next to $50. "That one's worth a little something. There may be some money here to help you with that fundraiser."

But this book is priceless. I imagine getting rid of it and feel the tears coming on again.

"I don't know. We'll see." I put the dust jacket back on and tuck it under my arm. A *lot* of these books can go, but more often than not, spending time in this room full of memories, turns me into an emotional mess. Maybe that's why I can't imagine letting anyone else organize it.

"C'mere." He pulls me into a hug that makes me melt. A hug just because. I guess I must look as out of sorts as I feel.

"It's hard," I whisper. "I just need a minute."

If I keep moving, I can stay one step ahead of change, the bad change at least. I can push it to a good change instead.

"Take all the time you need. I'm here," he says.

For now, I think. Everything is just for now, for this moment. Time seems like . . .

"Sometimes it feels like everything I love is slipping away."

My throat closes, and the tears fall in hot, silent rivers down my cheek.

He hugs me tighter, like he's saying *he* won't slip away, but I know that's not true. Of course he will. He's only visiting for a little while.

If loving someone with memory issues has taught me anything, it's to accept *now* for what it is, a gift. I want to soak up my time with Rom while I can and treasure every moment like it could be our last. Because soon enough, it will be.

Chapter Seven
Rom

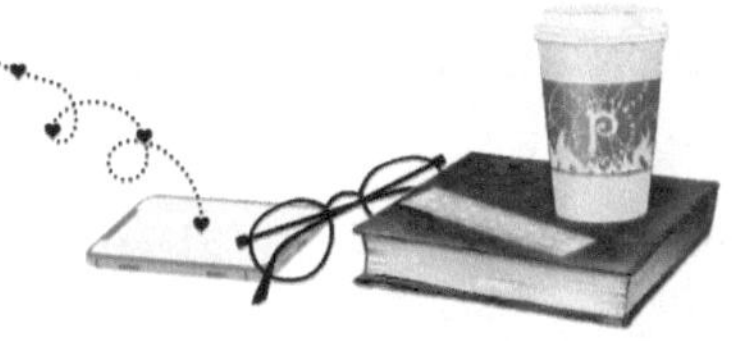

Y ou've got a lot on your shoulders." I smooth my hand up and down her back. "I have some ideas about these books, if you'll let me help you—"

"Miss Goode! Miss Goode!" Three tiny demons rush into the room with wide eyes, looking at the messy stacks of books everywhere.

"Ah ah ah, no kiddos in this room." Noelle wipes her eyes quickly and pastes on a smile, twisting on her skates to shoo them out the door. "Time for class."

We make our way to the front desk as they tug at her shirt and try to peer into her supply bags. She does a spin in her skates for them, swishing the goodies above her head. With a little wave to me, she's leading them in song to the *Little Critters* sitting area, like the cutest pied piper I've ever seen.

It's clear she's an amazing head librarian, but what a gut punch to hear about her uncle. No wonder she's on the verge of tears trying to deal with that and keep this old library running.

I see the *Returns* sign and the realization hits me. *Shoot!* The books I need to bring back are still in the car. If I want to check out more, I'll need to return those first.

On my walk back from the overpriced parking lot with my books in hand, a familiar voice rasps to my right.

"You really fucked up."

I spin to find Old Ethel in the alley behind her store, smoking with her face toward the sky. Demons love the sun — *the first fire in the darkness*. We soak up its heat like the cold-blooded creatures all the terrible tales said we were in ancient times.

I pause and wonder if she was even talking to me, but when I move to keep walking, she peeks at me with one blood-red eye.

"Number one rule in winning a woman over? Don't *fuck* them over first." She cranes her weathered face back to the sun with a pleased smile. "I suppose that puts me closer to winning our little bet, huh? $500 does sound nice."

"Fuck her over? You mean Noelle?" Who cares about that dumb bet I made with her the other day about dating Noelle.

She flicks her ash in a dusty arc. "Renting the building right out from under her constitutes that, I'd say."

The new Perkatory?

"What does she want that building for?" I'm utterly lost. "I know she's got a fundraiser, but there's no way she's expanding the library to the neighboring building."

Noelle made it clear she's struggling with her budget, and it's apparent enough from the inside — old posters, weathered carpet, the same musty furniture since I was a kid.

"She wanted to *move* the library," Old Ethel says. "Start fresh."

"What? Why?" It physically pains me to think of the library being anywhere but that old building on the corner. If it wasn't there, my memories would be nothing but a figment of my imagination. The best days of my childhood would have no home.

"Who knows?" She shrugs. "That girl's been making a big fuss about this fundraiser for months now."

My jaw sets as I move a step closer, growling. "And you gave her two measly dollars for her trouble, I noticed. Big help."

She points her long cigarette at me. "Demons don't give anything away for free, especially money."

I sigh and fist my hands at my hips. She's just like my parents. It's not that demonkind aren't charitable. It's just that most of us are raised to think that asking for donations comes across as weak. Poorly thought out. Bad business. But I know how Noelle thinks, and it's not a bad thing. She assumes everyone is willing to give the shirt off their back just like she would.

"Well, thanks for nothing then." I wave at her and walk back to the library, stopping in front of my empty coffee shop. The new Perkatory. Proof my family has really made it as a national chain by coming back to the small town we had nothing in. I realize now it was probably a point of pride for my parents to show everyone here that we made it.

But guilt eats at me. The numbers don't lie. I know this place will be a huge boon to the local community. If anything, Perkatory should bring more people to the library.

Why did she want *this* lease? The building is half the square footage of the library. It has a lot of modern upgrades, and if she has some new vision for the library, I guess I can understand the appeal of starting fresh.

Maybe it's the increased rent she mentioned. That's a shitty reason to downsize. Doesn't feel right. Noelle's always been sentimental, and she clearly takes her family's history maintaining the library in *that* building seriously.

I pick up my phone and call Mr. Jones, the real estate agent who settled the lease with me. He confirms that Noelle's been trying to rent the new Perkatory location for months, but her budget was way below their lowest acceptable monthly rate. The way he laughs at her negotiation attempts sets my teeth on edge.

He confirms the other available buildings in town were already either snatched up or don't fit her needs. The old library building she's in is owned by a large real estate conglomerate he gives me the name of.

I grumble a polite goodbye and hang up.

My hackles are up. People think they can push her around? It's total bullshit.

I make a call to her landlord. After some patience, I'm connected with the account manager for their real estate holdings in this area.

"We have a long-term tenant in place but always open to offers," they say in a chipper tone.

I huff, irritated they'd work behind her back like that. "I passed by the building today looking for a new site for my national brand, but it could really use some work. The best I can offer is half off the price on your site."

"That's below a threshold we're prepared to negotiate."

"Your loss." I hang up.

Sure, it's rude and yeah, I'm bluffing. I know the building's old but otherwise have no idea the state of it. That wasn't the point. I want to set them on edge, get them thinking the building isn't worth the higher rate they're demanding of Noelle. That way, if she does want to negotiate, it's an opening.

I shoot off a quick email to my lawyer and ask her to dig into the specifics of the existing building. It's a historic property. There's got to be rules and regulations around maintenance of those. I don't know anything about her budget, but information is the best asset in business, and if I can help her, I will.

With my stack of books under my arm, I march back to the library, intent on getting to the bottom of all this fundraiser business.

Noelle's musical voice drifts from the backroom, reminding me she's in the middle of a class.

I loiter near the front table decorated with a mini evergreen tree, mistletoe, and a few candle holders representing various human winter holidays. There are decorations for some fae and orc traditions as well, but the table is dominated by a red and yellow display. The Advent of the Honest, demonkind's most sacred holiday, is a two-week long affair that ends on New Year's Eve.

So many beliefs and cultures are grouped together on one festive little table.

This is what a library can do — celebrate everything all at once. It's a place where treasures are kept on display, never hoarded and always shared. Anyone can pick a book up off the shelf and expand their mind or find a cozy place to reread an old favorite.

A stack of her fliers sits on the edge of the table. I pick one up.

Fundraiser! Save Our Library!

I place my books next to the *Returns* sign at the end of the counter. The demon girl behind the circulation desk doesn't seem in a chatty mood anyway. I walk back to the Little

Critters area. Like the rest of this town, everything looks the same but so much smaller, more precious somehow, now that I know it's all in jeopardy.

Noelle's back is to me as she reads a book to the dozen or more kids sitting cross-legged on the threadbare circular rug. Most of them are demonkind, which twists my heart in the best way. I guess not every demon family is as single-minded as my parents were in enforcing a business-only education, not that I can fault them for it. They were doing their best.

The story she narrates is about a horse exploring the ocean, one of our favorites growing up. The kids all look up at her with stars in their eyes. I know the feeling. Hearing her narrate a book is pure magic. Her hands move in dramatic arcs and each character gets a unique, dramatic voice. She embodies their emotions so well, taking us on a journey with her, pausing with dramatic effect right at a climactic scene.

Noelle has always understood what makes stories so important. Adventure. Connection. Self-growth.

For me, books were usually a means of escape. First, from the pain of recovering from my injuries while I was in the hospital. Then, my loneliness as a child living with scars that made others stare. I like being alone, always have. In that way, this library was my sanctuary, a place I wasn't just the demon boy with thick glasses and an ugly face. I could get lost and be someone new for a few hours.

Making friends with Noelle changed everything. I started to see books for what they could teach me, how I could understand people and the world around me differently.

This library is important. It can't fail. The town needs it too much.

What the library needs, what Noelle needs, is support to grow stronger, not a place she has to shrink to fit.

She sets the book down and moves on to craft time, passing out supplies to each kid. When she talks them through the day's craft, making a braided bookmark, I get choked up.

"The holidays are just around the corner!" She ruffles two boys' dark hair between their horns. They must be twins. She moves to separate a nearby gaggle who are fighting over supplies. "There's enough for everyone, and you only need three colors. Use the safety scissors! We have twenty minutes left of class, so focus kiddos. Make as many as your fast little fingers can braid. These are gifts everyone will love. Make them for your parents or siblings or even your best friend, anyone who needs a reminder of how special they are to you."

Emotion burns in me, wishing I could turn back time and never leave this town. But I also know that's impossible. Fate turned out differently, and we are who we are for a reason.

We reconnected at this moment in time for a reason.

I turn around and walk out of the library.

Could I wait until Noelle's class is over and steal a moment of her time in between her other ten tasks? Absolutely. I've got nothing to do today.

Am I going to? Absolutely not.

I came to Winter Bliss to open a coffee shop, but that's not what really matters right now.

When I get to my car, the flier is fisted in my hand. I flatten it on the dash and pull up my phone, depositing another $100 to her fundraiser and drafting a text.

Whether she'd ever be interested in me romantically or not, friends look out for each other. I have business acumen that can help her. I know it. But I don't think Noelle will stop moving long enough to tell me about what's really going on with the library unless I get her alone.

She and I need to have a little chat.

Chapter Eight

Noelle

"The sun goddess Enrama closed her golden eyes and fell into a deep sleep. Daylight faded from the land. The sky bled to night until nothing more than shadows danced in the cold, damp black.

Only Mother Darkness remained.

"My clever children," she whispered from the deep, "you saved yourselves with the truth."

The kids sitting cross-legged around me stare up, wide-eyed and quiet for the first time since we started class. We've reached the end of a traditional story most of them have heard countless times around the winter holidays. The Advent of the Honest, otherwise known as New Year's Eve, is the night most demons believe Mother Darkness stopped the death of the world. Demonkind upheld an important bargain with her, and she promised that the darkest day would not be the end and that every year the light would return. Like many myths across time, it coincides with natural phenomena, this one being winter solstice and the new year.

"Her black claws stretched over the land. With molten drops from each sharp tip, she placed the mountains where she willed. Fires from the deepest earth surged forth. Light and heat flooded the land once more. It was the longest night before a new beginning, and Mother Darkness left them with her last words."

I raise my hands like a conductor and play-act my deepest, spookiest voice.

"Fair is fair and . . ."

I pause. They all know the last words.

"A deal is a deal!" the kids shout.

I clap for them. This is why I love my job. These kids. All the community programs that bring people together. I skate around the room to clean up the last of the supplies and shepherd them to their parents. By the time they're out the door, I realize what I'm missing.

Rom.

He left?

I swallow down the emotion in my throat, looking toward the front window. Suddenly, I'm fourteen years old again and my best friend disappeared without a word. It took weeks for my uncle to figure out they'd moved out of state. No one knew how to contact them. That was a dark winter break, the first time I'd ever felt truly alone. My best friend was just . . . gone. It was my first heartbreak, really —

one that led me to guard my heart with thicker walls than most.

My phone rings.

Ugh, another contractor. With a frown, I answer and listen to the breakdown of how much it will cost to get the foundation repaired and the roof replaced. Their quote is more than the entire fundraising goal I had for a move and still doesn't address a few other repairs needed or the increased rent. I head back to the circulation desk, deflated.

"A handsomely dressed demon was asking after you," my uncle teases, peeking over the book he's reading. His statement tells me he doesn't remember who Rom is like last time.

I play it cool and shrug.

"He picked up a flier." My uncle raises and lowers his eyebrows. "Maybe he needs a book delivery."

"Oh. Maybe," I say. He grabbed a flier? My belly flutters. I check my texts and sure enough, there's a message. Rom's $100 donation puts the fundraiser goal over the $1,000 mark. He mentions how he had to leave early. I imagine opening a store means there's plenty keeping him busy. But still, he wants more books, and not just any books, books from me. A story about magic and friendship. Gah, why is he just the best?

"It's nice to see you smile like that, Noey." My uncle pokes me with a long ruler. "Who is this guy?"

I grab a sharpie and color in the fundraiser chart near the front door, debating how to answer the question. *He's the best friend that broke my heart when he left town.* I don't want to probe old memories that could confuse Uncle Darren and only bring down the holiday cheer.

"He's opening a coffee shop next door." It sounds so nice and quaint. A small-town romance novel. But life is messier than that, at least mine is.

I dart around the library, getting things finished so we can close early and send everyone home by lunch. Tomorrow is Christmas Eve, and we'll be closed for three days, not that I'll have much of a break. I need to hunker down and do research on other contractors to call, as well as prep a million things for the festival coming up. Once I get a handle on the cost of all the repairs, I have to update the fundraiser page to increase the goal amount.

But first, book deliveries. I have two local drop offs, then it's up Last Hour Road to Rom's cabin. It'll be a nice drive. We had a couple days of heavy snow followed by wet flurries, but now the sun is shining and the weather's pleasant.

"Eat this." A PB&J slides in front of me. Uncle Darren's cure-all combination of protein, carbs, and fat.

"Thanks," I mumble as I dig in.

I've been running around like a chicken with my head cut off the last few days. There's not a single other rental in town that would work for the library since the smaller building next door is already leased. I'll just have to try to make this old building work.

My mind races. It's so overwhelming, I don't even know where to start.

The fundraiser is the only thing that can save us now. We're lucky, in a way, because New Year's Eve is the biggest, busiest day in town. In eight days, demons from all over the region will flock to Winter Bliss for the day-long Truthfire Festival. With so many tourists in town, I know if I can get a handle on the monetary goal and make our fundraiser table great, I can raise what the library needs to get back on its feet.

After checking our emails, rather than do the 200 things on my scattered to-do lists, I casually cyberstalk Rom. Sometimes I embrace mental distraction over mental disaster. Sue me.

BeastlyandBookish. Adorable, misguided demon.

His social media feed is so aesthetically pleasing. Warm tones with hot drinks, showing off his eyeglasses and beautiful books. Just an hour ago, he uploaded a glowing review of the books I leant him. *The politics of power extend from leadership to the bedroom in this engrossing read.* I bite back a smile at his intellectual assessment of the spicy scenes.

I keep scrolling. Every time a book comes into frame, I barely notice the cover. All I see are his hands — strong, thick fingers, veins for days. It's practically pornographic. No wonder he has over twenty thousand followers and dozens of thirsty comments on each post. I scroll and scroll but never see his face. When I search his real name on the internet, only a few photos pop up, mostly with his family for business events. He's usually in the back, doing his best to hide away.

"What else do you need from us?" My uncle looms over my shoulder, joined by Fran and Than, my two student workers who work full-time over the holidays and part-time during high school semesters. The orc supervisor of the memory care facility is also a few steps away, and they're all staring.

I click off the screen and clear my throat.

"Oh, not much else to do." It's a white lie. Ten things drift into my mind of little chores around the library, but I hate to bother them. "You guys take off."

They look at each other.

"I'll usher everybody out," Uncle Darren says.

"That's a great idea. I'll help." The lady from the facility loops her arm through his with a reassuring squeeze. "Our group is loading up in the van now."

"I'll sweep and close down the second floor." Fran says. Talk about someone who would love Rare Books. I bet I'd have to tear my introverted demon assistant out of there if I reopened the section.

"I'll shelve that last cart before locking up," Than says. He's a super responsible kid. They both are. I gave them keys to the place for times like this when I'm in and out and everywhere all at once.

"*You* head out early." Fran glares at me. Her facial piercings and dark red eyes should be fearsome, but she's just adorable when she's serious, which is basically all the time.

"We've got this." Than smiles at me.

I give them a sheepish smile and grab my coat. "Thanks, guys."

In a blur, my two in-town deliveries are done, and I'm up Last Hour Road and standing at Rom's front door.

"He's only here for another week and a half," I whisper under my breath, remembering how I impulsively kissed him, how his hug felt better than anything I've felt from a man in years, and how being alone with him is like catnip for me. "You're busy. It's a bad idea to get too close. Friends. We can be friends."

The door creaks open a sliver. Rom's face and the darkened arch of his broken horn comes into view.

"You okay?" he asks.

Why does his voice have to be so sexy? Ah, I'm being a complete headcase standing here whispering to myself. I heave out a huge exhale. "Sorry. Yes. It's just been such a long week, if I'm honest."

"Let's talk about it." He opens the door, dressed smartly in an argyle sweater, gray slacks, and his signature eyeglasses. Gosh, he's a librarian's wet dream, I swear.

I sit on a cozy little loveseat in the living area while Rom makes us herbal tea. He peppers me with questions about the fundraiser, and I start to explain all the repairs that need to be made. I know I'm rambling. My chest gets tight when I talk too fast, going down a new rabbit hole about the plumbing issues in the downstairs bathroom.

A teacup slides into my hands, stilling them and reminding me to breathe.

"Thanks." My thumb finds a small crack in the lip, not a sharp or recent accident. The edges are smooth, the colors a little faded. I bet it's Miss Ethel's favorite cup. "Cute."

He settles beside me, a thick-necked giant of a demon circling a tiny spoon in his teacup. "Oh, it's broken? I can get you another one."

I wrap both hands around it. "No. He's mine, and I love him. The chip adds character."

His mouth curves in the tiniest smile as he passes me the honey in silence. He must remember my sweet tooth. I feel a blush heat my cheeks. This is so weird. We were the best of friends as kids, but now we're adults who live across the country from each other. Perfect strangers who know how the other likes their tea.

I can't let my mind run away with fantasies of him staying in Winter Bliss. He's a successful businessman from a big city who's only here to open a coffee shop. He has much bigger fish to fry in life.

At the same time, I won't deny that sitting here with a friend in a cute little cabin high above the town that's been running me ragged isn't a nice break. It is. It's nice to have someone ask about *my* problems and really listen.

"Have you spoken to a bank about a business loan?" he asks, sipping his tea. "You could pay it back over time."

"Oh, I wouldn't know where to start with that."

"I'm happy to help."

I make a farting sound with my lips and wave him off. I don't want to be a bother. It's the holidays, and he's got his own business to get up and running.

"The increase in rent is a cost you could negotiate." He sets his tea on the table and turns more toward me, his knee brushing along the length of my leg. Oh, he smells nice, like herbs and soap. "They aren't paying for repairs of a historic building, so there might be a way to press them on the issue."

"I don't know." I trace the gilded curve of the tea plate back and forth. "It seems fair to have me pay for repairs since we've rented this building for decades."

"Exactly my point. You've paid your fair share of rent. It seems fair to *me* that the owner of the building maintains it and that money should go toward repairs."

"I'll just, uh . . ." I imagine trying to convince my landlord to do the repairs again over the phone and remember how quickly they dismissed the last request I made. "I'll focus on the fundraiser."

He's trying to help, I know. I just hate rocking the boat.

"Onward and upward." I give him a smile that must not be convincing, judging by the concerned slant of his mouth. "The fundraiser is going great thanks to your support! Speaking of, let me get you those books."

I pull out the young adult duology I picked up for him and hold both covers up with a waggle.

He grins. "That series is one of my favorites."

My face falls. "You've already read it?"

"And her other trilogy in that same world. I collect all the special editions that pop up. I probably have six different versions of these two books."

"Oh." I frown.

"But . . ." He leans forward and plucks them from my grasp, tracing the edge of the hardcover. "It's been a few years since they came out, and I've never re-read them back-to-back. No time like the present. This was an excellent choice."

"Oh." I grin, feeling light and happy at the compliment. "Thanks. Good."

He twists the first book around, reading the summary on the back. "You know, I've always loved the heist and plot twists of these books, but I never really considered how at their heart, the stories are about friendship."

A book about magic and friendship is what he asked for. I realize all of a sudden how most of the friends later become love interests. Welp.

"And found family," I croak. "One of my favorite tropes."

"It's kind of crazy how even though we haven't talked in years, you pick one of my favorite books." He leans his beefy arm against the back of the couch and rests his head on his fist, staring at me with disarming warmth. "You always had a knack for that. Your special talent."

My cheeks flame. I pluck the bookmark I tucked into the book out and hand it to him. "I made you this in the Little Critters class today."

I hold my breath, wondering if he remembers the friendship bookmark I gave him when we were kids. His lips part, eyes dancing over the simple design of braided threads. He clutches it to his chest and looks at me with bright eyes before turning to pick up a book from a side table behind him.

It has a pretty gold foiled cover of vines and thorns, but it's what's poking out of the middle that catches my eye. He pulls it out and hands it to me.

Tears cloud my vision.

"You still have it?" The years between when I made the bookmark and now seem obvious in the frayed ends and faded color, but the design is just like I remember.

Mountains and snow and Rom and Noelle.

"I'm not even sure I could do this design again. I lost the instructional book shortly after you uh . . ." I look up at him, my breaths short. ". . . you left."

A moment stretches between us, full of so many things unsaid.

There are no words that could make our friendship whole again, cross the space of time and distance between who we were and who we are now. Yet *here* we are, close enough I can smell his aftershave and feel the heat of him.

A siren blares outside somewhere. Familiar. I don't hear it often, but it's a loud, distinctive sound you never forget. My skin prickles with alarm.

"Avalanche," I whisper.

Rom's hands grip my arms.

"We're high up," I say. "But this cabin is right on a cliff. If we're in its path, we could be crushed. We could be pushed right off." I'm talking a mile a minute as my mind races. An avalanche?! The only thing grounding me is where his skin meets mine. "Does the cabin have a basement?"

A strange creaking sound comes from outside. The rush of snow.

"No." His eyes swirl orange, sparkling with a golden emotion I can't read.

"It's not safe outside. We shouldn't move," I choke out.

"Okay." He draws me onto his lap, eyes flaring solid gold. It feels so natural, so right, and I cling to him, burrowing in. He curls over me, leaning his face and horns between me and the ceiling, caging me with his body. "I'll keep you safe."

I believe him. It's illogical, completely crazy. He can't save me or himself if an avalanche comes down on top of us, but his fierce gaze tells me how much he'd try. I try to breathe, but it's like getting air into someone else's body. Every inhale is labored, heavy and measured.

The sirens sing out, and each passing note, each breath, each moment, could be my last.

Is this it, the end? Is this how I go? If it is, this is how I'd want to go, held fast in the arms of someone who looks at me like I'm the only thing that matters even when the world is ending.

I shouldn't feel safe with him, but I do. He's here. The first boy who stole my heart. The first man who's made me feel alive in years.

The house shakes. There's a rumbling outside, but the blood roaring in my ears is louder.

We're alive. Right now, we're alive, but for how much longer?

This is all we have.

I arch back. My nose rubs against his, and I inhale. His scent is driving me crazy. Our lips are so close, our breaths shared in this sweet, sacred space. I don't know who closes the distance, only that we crash together. His arms band around me, one hand cradling my head as he groans and shifts. He's everywhere all at once, a force of nature seizing me tight. Keeping me safe.

His mouth claims mine. The kiss is like a fight where we're both on the same side. Our tongues slide, teeth bite at lips, desperate for more of the other. More and more. Nothing's ever felt like this. Hot and soft and needy and hard all at the same time. My fingers trace over his scarred cheek, delighting in each textured inch. He groans and sucks at my bottom lip. Gasping for air, his mouth slides over my heated skin, my ear, and down my neck. I trace up his spine all the way to his silky hair, feeling him shiver. His horns are in my hands. My fingers feel the smooth edges of the broken one, trailing down to the scars from his temple to his lip; the scars he's lived with since this mountain nearly killed him as a kid.

An irrational thought hits me. If anyone could survive the dangers of this mountain, it's Rom. He's done it once before. Perhaps fate or his gods or whatever he believes in is with him today.

Greedy for more of his mouth, I grip the base of one horn and scratch my nails along his scalp to lead his face back to mine. He's hard beneath me, an insistent, hot presence between my aching thighs. Just right. A perfect fit. I can't help but rock and slide, a wet mess already, and it makes his exhales shudder. Between softer kisses, I marvel at his face. Each dash of my lips makes him softer somehow. He's no one else's picture of ideal male beauty, but he's mine. Every misaligned bone and scar. Those kiss-bitten lips and glittering eyes.

Mine.

He blinks in surprise. Oh dear, I said that out loud.

I pant, the sound of my breaths overloud in my ears. His grip on me is ironclad and as hard as the cock underneath me. When he shifts, the couch groans. That's when I realize what's changed. It's so quiet.

The sirens have stopped.

The avalanche is over.

We're alive.

Chapter Nine
Rom

"We should go outside and see what happened." Noelle hops out of my lap and paces near the front door, shaking out her hands.

We almost died. Maybe? And she kissed me again. What was that?

"We're so lucky, oh my goodness. Maybe we can see where the avalanche struck." Her head whips to me, a picture of panic with flushed cheeks, pink mouth, and messy hair. She's so pretty it's hard to concentrate. "What if someone needs our help?"

I exhale and scrub a hand down my face, leaning forward on my knees. *Mine*, she'd said. About me! And she meant it. I think. At that moment, she didn't look crazed. But now she's up and tracing frantic circles in the front rug, and I don't know what to make of any of it.

Surely, it was all just adrenaline. Panic. Hormones. *She doesn't date outsiders*, Old Ethel said. And Noelle is so beautiful, she'd have her pick of guys. Who do I think I am? I blow out a heavy breath, wishing the wild, sexy moment we had would fizzle out of my system, but the undercurrent of heat won't leave me. My body is humming and fired up.

"I need a second," I growl out and crack my neck, letting my hands stroke up my horns and down, chasing away the tingle her soft touch left behind. It made me crazy when she grabbed me like that. I'm still catching my breath, pushing down the heady sensations, when I realize how quiet she is. Noelle isn't a quiet person. I peek up, and she bites her lip.

"I'm sorry," she peeps.

"Don't be sorry." I shake my head, feeling more in control of whatever took hold of me when I knew we were in danger, when she melted in my arms, and when she said I was hers. She needs me here, in the present, just as much as I need her. "Whatever you feel, please don't be sorry. I'm not."

"Okay," she says, so quiet I almost don't hear it.

I stand and readjust myself. The erection may be another minute or two. She glances down at it, then to the window, her fiery red hair like a curtain sweeping back. I want to touch her again so badly, but we're in the middle of a natural disaster. I need to get my mind off my turbulent emotions and take stock of our situation.

Our safety. Noelle's safety. I promised her that. I was prepared for the roof to fall on top of me and just cage her with my body and horns. If she had a chance to survive, that was going to be my end, and I was okay with it.

"Alright, let's look around outside."

I change into some warmer clothes, and she shrugs on her coat. As we head out the front door, I stay as close to her as is respectful, wanting to bundle her in my arms again but knowing it's not logical or useful to our mission.

Within seconds, my lungs fill with the frigid air. It's like every last inch of my insides is sharpening and waking up. We walk to the edge of the deck. Though Old Ethel's property is unaffected, and the road is clear near us, the damage is evident.

The avalanche missed us by a good way but is still close enough to see. A giant white slash of snow cuts across Last Hour Road where it snakes down the mountain below us. The snowdrift has to be at least ten feet tall. Only the top of a tall road sign peeks out, and the mound slopes even higher.

It's horrifying but beautiful. I drag a handful of snow from the railing, watching it melt in my fiery fingertips. Snow seems so harmless, a soft nothing dripping to the ground. But the quiet all around us is unnerving, like the avalanche snuffed out all life that used to exist below that fresh, perfect snow. I glance to the dark trees off to the side and shiver, already wanting to be back inside.

"That's a relief." Noelle sighs, tucking her hair behind her ears, gone wild in the whipping wind. "There aren't any cabins in its path as far as I know."

"Nature is crazy." I clear my throat, the cold making it hard to breathe suddenly. An unwelcome memory of my accident as a kid grips me, how I tumbled down this very mountain out hiking in a dangerous section of slippery rocks.

"I'm stuck," she says.

I look at her feet, confused. She's stuck in the snow? Her head snaps back to the blocked road below. The reality of the situation hits me. Noelle is stuck with me. Maybe for days. Sweet Mother Darkness, this is a holiday miracle. I can feel my grin stretch wide.

"I'm stuck!" she sobs.

Oh no.

"I have to go." She darts off and into the woods at the side of the property.

"Wait! What?" I chase after her. The trees don't let as much snow gather on the ground, and we're near the top of the mountain, so I'm not worried about another avalanche. But if she strays too far—

"There's a path downhill just over here," she shouts over her shoulder. I can barely make out her rambling as I try to catch up. "I'm sure I could get back home that way. There's too much to do, Rom. You don't understand. I can't be stuck up here. Avalanches take so long to clear. A couple years ago, the people in cabins up here were stuck for weeks."

She scampers through the forest, sniffling and crying between statements.

Anxiety starts to creep into my thoughts. "Slow down, Noelle."

"The Truthfire Festival is in a week! It's my last chance to save the library!"

I'm still several feet behind her, struggling to catch up as the sharp, chilled air stings down to my lungs. The snow crunching underfoot gives way to hard ground then moss-covered rocks.

Everything is different here. No, *familiar*.

She stops at a fern-covered wall. Rivulets of hot water flow down the stone face. Noelle tests her footing on a lower boulder, like she's going to climb down.

My body flashes cold. A lead stone sinks in my gut.

She cannot be serious about going down the mountain this way. I remember this area, flashes of it at least. It's a treacherous route.

Pockets of hot springs and waterfalls dot this side of the mountain. The air is thick with warm humidity. Boiling water burbles up and streams down the cliffs, feeding waterways leading to the biggest waterfall of all. It's picturesque but dangerous for climbing, no matter the time of year. Featured on postcards for the town, it flows straight out of the mountain accompanied by a cloud of piping hot steam, giving the lake its name.

"Tell me you're not hiking down to Teapot Lake from here."

"Do you like being lied to?" She gets a defiant look on her face that would be cute if I wasn't so terrified.

"Absolutely not." I realize that sounds like an answer to her question instead of what I meant. "You are *not* going down there."

"I'll be careful." Her eyes go round and placating, but she looks down the steep cliff, and I can see the hesitation. Her fingers feel around the rocks and slip in the vegetation, finding no firm hold. "I know my way."

She did bring me that map. I don't remember a lot of specifics of the mountain, but I know *this* section is a popular place local daredevil kids like to visit. They can slide on their butts down a few sections of hot springs, which also makes it extremely dangerous.

"This path is a tangle of wet rocks, geysers, and lava pits, Noelle." I've been here and paid the price. My vision narrows to where she's trying to pick her way down a cliff face. This isn't even the most dangerous section, and she's already slipping.

"I'll be fine!" she says, not even looking at me, focused on trying to navigate boulders topped with sharp edges. She's close but too far away for me to grab.

"No you won't!" I roar. My chest is heaving. "It's a path only dumb kids take."

She whips around, clearly offended, until she sees me.

Anger and frustration boils out of me, but the fear is hotter. Even though it's not the same exact spot, the terrain brings unwelcome memories crashing down. The day I tumbled down this mountain. Pain. Burning gashes. Broken bones and blood. I was with my brothers doing a risky hike up the lava channels on a dare. Never the most athletic, I scrambled to catch up.

One stupid slip left me scarred for life.

I struggle to breathe as the memories take on a new life. Noelle falling. Noelle screaming. Her red hair tangled in dirt. Her perfect face covered in scars like mine.

"You're okay."

Her voice cuts through the fog in my mind. I don't see her, but I feel her hand in mine. I crush her to me and struggle through shuddered breaths.

"You're okay," she repeats. Her hands rub up and down my back. Her cheek lays against my heart. "You're safe. Everything's okay. Try to breathe."

"Don't go down there." My whisper is hoarse and cracked.

She exhales, her breath hot and sweet against my chest. "You're right. It was a bad idea."

"This mountain is dangerous." I squeeze her tight and come back to the present, shake my head, and focus on what's in front of me. She's alright. My hand smooths down her soft hair. My knuckles drag down her cheek.

She's not hurt. She's whole and safe. I try to go for a joke to lighten the mood. "I'll follow you down this razor-sharp, slip 'n slide volcano if that's where you're going, but I think my scars prove I've got zero instincts for the venture."

She pulls back and smiles, but I can tell it's a courtesy. She's still worried about me.

"I know you're a tough, capable woman, but you wouldn't put me in danger like that would you?"

Her gaze is soft as she studies me. I feel strung tight and a thousand things at once — weak as a lamb, heart racing with leftover anxiety, but also ready to do anything necessary to protect her.

"Stay with me," I say, then reword as a question. "You'll stay until the road is clear?" I don't know if my body will let go of her until she agrees.

She lays her chin against my chest and nods. My breath whooshes out in relief. Okay, that's settled.

We hold each other for a few moments, just coming down from the stress. Then I remember why she ran away in the first place.

"This fundraiser for the library," I say. "I caught some of what you said, but I take it that's your main concern?"

Her eyes tighten, worry coloring her expression. "Yeah. The building needs so many repairs. I have to get quotes to increase the fundraising goal and figure out what to do for the library's table at the festival. There will be so many tourists with deep pockets. I just know it's my last chance. I can't be stuck here for a week. I can't. New Year's Eve is in eight days."

"A week is a long time," I say, measuring the days out in my mind. She has time. "The library is closed for a couple days because of the holiday, right?"

"Right," she says.

"So for right now, at least a few days, you're not allowed to worry." I release the hug but grab her hand in an iron grip, leading us away from the rocky area.

"Easier said than done," she says, waving her free hand in the air. I just know she's gearing up for another rant. "But I've got about a hun—"

"Wait," I interrupt. "Will you let me help you?"

"Uhhh." She wrings her hands together.

"I'll take notes and draft up a project plan including everything the library needs for repairs and everything you need for the fundraiser." My mind clicks into work mode. General manager reporting for duty. If I'm good at one thing, it's doing the least amount of work for the highest reward. She doesn't need eight days. This is easy work if we plan and work as a team. Whether it's staff schedules or speed reading, I'm an expert at using my time efficiently. "We'll estimate costs, timelines, and discuss delegation."

"Oh. Wow. That sounds nice," she says.

I get the sense Noelle doesn't ask for help much. She may command a team of volunteers at the library, but I'd bet my bottom dollar she does the lion's share of the work day in and day out.

"It is nice. You'll see." I smile back at her and pull up my phone, then groan when I see I have no connection. "Ugh, the service here is so spotty."

"Oh! It's way better at the top of that ridge."

I grimace at the snowy hillside from here to there. It seems we're either braving avalanches or dangerous cliffs.

"It's safe," she says, squeezing my hand. "There's a path through a burnt-out section of woods all the way up to the top, maybe half a mile or so. You never went up to Frostwing Lookout as a kid?"

I was fourteen when we left town, only halfway through my freshman year. Frostwing Lookout was the scenic spot the older high school kids went to to make out. I shake my head and can't help but wonder who she's been up here with. What friends replaced me? What boyfriends broke her heart?

Putting my melancholy thoughts aside, I refocus. She leads the way up the mountain as I pepper her with logistical questions about her fundraiser and repairs needed. The path is flat and clear, so I can take notes and make a simple project plan in my spreadsheet app as we go. When we reach the top, the list is complete, but the details still need work. We settle on a long, flat rock as she looks it over.

The air is cold but crisp and the wind whips around so fast I keep an arm around her, still a little on edge from the avalanche and the thought of her in danger.

Up here, though, everything feels better. Falcons careen in the evening sky. It's nearly sunset and the fading light shines a golden warmth over everything. The white topped mountains and valleys are something I haven't really seen in years. Snow makes everything new.

Even the avalanche seems like a brushstroke from a god this high up, the road and dozens of uprooted trees simply playthings that were painted over. How easy it was to wipe away something that grew for hundreds of years. Gone in a flash. A sense of fearlessness and humility wash over me, both at the same time.

"It looks achievable all laid out like that." She takes my phone and in the "Assign to" column for each action item starts typing her name. Over and over in every box.

"No." I pluck the phone out of her grasp. "If I'm helping you, I'm helping. And I have people who help me, so we're taking some of these action items. Are you telling me you don't have volunteers who can sort books or buy a table-cloth, a pallet of bottled water, and a ream of paper?"

She narrows her eyes. "Fine. I'll ask someone to do that."

I bump her shoulder. "No need to get pouty. There's still plenty you can do."

We spend the next few minutes divvying up the work until we get to the last line, which is probably the most important. I really want to take it off her plate.

"About this one, signing a new lease." I point it out to her. "Can I look into it first?"

"My lease? I have to sign it ASAP. The new rate starts on January 1st. I was planning to call them right now to see if I can agree over the phone somehow."

"Give me a few days."

"Why?"

"Most of your fundraising goal which is currently around—" I double check the sum figure "—$15,000 is going toward physical repairs of the building itself."

She nods, grimacing. "It's so much. I didn't think it would be that high."

"In my opinion, you shouldn't be responsible for any of it."

"The landlord is?" she asks but looks profoundly uncomfortable. The last time I mentioned this, she said she felt it was fair she paid, but it's not.

"I'd like your permission to speak with them as well as secure three bids for each of your bigger repair needs. You shouldn't be on the hook for any of that since you don't own the property but presenting professional estimates to the landlord can only help the case. I don't know how they're getting away with neglecting basic upkeep of a historic property. They could be fined. Big time."

"That sounds really messy." Her leg shakes against my knee. I place my hand on it and squeeze, hating how uncomfortable she looks.

"I understand." I exhale and try to control this burning need to take this off her. "How about this? Put me to work. Give me a deadline, a few days to look into the rent and repair estimates. I'd love to try to help you with this so you can focus on the festival."

She chews the inside of her mouth and studies me, but I think I see a little hope in her eyes.

"I don't like seeing you taken advantage of," I continue. "There's no reason you should be overcharged by contractors or even liable for repairs on a building you don't own while the owner tries to increase your rent for a building that's falling down around your ears."

"Fair point," she says.

"Can I make some calls?" I press my hands together in prayer, itching to get started. "Will you let me worry about the repairs and the rent for a few days?"

"Don't burn any bridges. They're all nice people."

"Persuasive but professional. I promise." I cross my heart and lift my pinky to hers. "Deal?"

"A deal is a deal." Her smile tucks over on one side of her face as she loops her pinky through mine and shakes. "You have until New Year's Eve, then I'm signing the lease no matter what."

"I won't let you down," I promise.

She sighs. "We never asked for help when things broke down because my uncle was always so handy. He tried calling the landlord, but it's such a big company that it's hard to get a response, you know? He just fixed it."

"Which wasn't fair to him, and it isn't fair to you."

"Yeah! They should take care of the building. It's a piece of local history."

"I agree."

"The town deserves better," she says.

"And so do you."

"You know, we always pay our rent on time. Every month."

"They'd be lucky to keep you as tenants."

"Exactly. We deserve respect."

"Always." I grin. It's nice to see her defending herself instead of other people for once. She seems to take on every possible responsibility, even ones that aren't hers, but I aim to change that. Life works out so well when you learn to trust and rely on others. I want to be that for her. At least, for now.

Noelle is a vision of flushed skin and indignance and bright red hair dancing in the wind. As much as I want to kiss her, I can't.

We have work to do.

Chapter Ten

Noelle

Is there anything sexier than true competence? Is that a kink?

Rom's broad frame stands in stark contrast to the rainbow-swirl sunset and the wild, winter landscape of snowy mountains. His dark hair and arching horns are a thing of beauty, even the broken one.

But it's not the visual aesthetics I find sexiest. It's the way he strides back and forth, working over the phone with laser-focused attention. And I have a lot of time to watch him since my list of things to do shrank to a very achievable handful of items. I begrudgingly handed over my few tasks to my two student workers.

I called Than's mom first, who helps out with the children's programming from time to time, but she roped her son in immediately and before I knew it, he'd called Fran and they were both chiming in in the background. When they heard about the avalanche, they were relieved I was okay and promised to let everyone know that I have a safe place to stay until the road clears. They assured me the library would be fine, even if it takes a few days for me to get back. But will it? I've had serious doubts the past few days, feeling like I was barely keeping everything together, like one wrong move would send my house of cards tumbling down.

Within two minutes of getting off my phone call and listening to Rom though, my hope is soaring like the white falcons above us that call this crag home. Rom in business mode is magnificent. A revelation.

"I absolutely agree. A fifteen percent proposed reduction in the rental rate seems more appropriate. It's unacceptable she's being treated like this."

He's trying to *lower* the cost of my lease? Only a demon would have that kind of audacity. I see it day in and day out around town, how they offer a price they know the other party won't accept as a way to meet in the middle. I've never been good at that, but Rom clearly is. He's *very* good. His authoritative tone has me hot and bothered, crossing and uncrossing my legs. I missed everything but the last bit of his conversation with his lawyer. On speakerphone, he furiously types as she shares legal insights, and he asks pointed questions in return.

"So the Idaho legislation requires inspection of heritage buildings every decade? When was that signed? Mmmhm.

And the fines are tiered? Who can make a complaint? Thanks, Blanca. Bill me double for the holiday."

After that call, he dials up one of his Perkatory supervisors from Austin who helps him with special projects. She has the sunniest disposition and doesn't seem put out by Rom's authoritative tone. He doesn't boss her around so much as treat her like a partner, and she seems excited to solicit three contractor bids for each repair project. She even suggests looking for out-of-town contractors willing to travel. That way, we have a wider pool of companies and can circumvent the higher prices in our small town.

"Brilliant. I owe you big time," he says into the receiver as he looks at me. "But do me a favor and prioritize contractors who can do the jobs as a package deal. Even if the bid is a little higher for one contractor over four, it may be worth it to make my friend's management of the projects easier."

His friend. God, I wish we could be more than that. But the flip side of listening to him in work mode is that it reminds me that people like Rom don't live in Winter Bliss. Nobody moves this fast or gets this much done. We aren't home to the rich and successful unless they're here for vacation or retirement.

We're a sleepy town. He'll get bored after a while. They always do.

My glum train of thought must be transparent on my face because as the call winds down, he comes over to fiddle with a lock of my hair. His thumb notches on my chin and lifts my face to the setting sun. I smile and so does he, as though our emotions connect through a tether.

Does he feel it too? We were best friends so long ago, but to me, that soul-deep connection hasn't changed at all. The more time I spend with him, the stronger that teenage crush grows again. Gah. I've been reading too many books from the romance section. I'm hopeless.

His next call is to my landlord, the mega-huge real estate company that never gives me a straight answer. Despite the snowy weather, I practically melt listening to his opening conversation. He's demanding and firm. His voice never softens, and he doesn't take no for an answer. He asks probing question after probing question. Any time the person on the other line falters, he demands to be connected to another level of management. When he makes eye contact with me, he flashes an encouraging smile before getting pulled back into the conversation.

After three transfers, he's speaking with the chief operating officer. Rom's demeanor turns firm and frankly, scary hot. He said he wouldn't burn bridges, but my word, I could never speak with this kind of bravado. The executive on the other line answers occasionally or asks a question of his own, but I can tell they're taking each statement seriously.

"I represent Miss Goode in all real estate matters and reviewed the offer for next year's rental lease. Via email and certified mail, we've submitted a counteroffer as well as a request for documentation of compliance with the state's legislative requirement for regular assessment of historic buildings. The package includes legal citations for your counsel to consider. It's important to note that in their twenty years of occupancy, the Goode family is unaware of any such assessment and have completed all necessary repairs themselves. That is untenable and puts your company at risk for both public safety and government fines. The building has been the area's epicenter for learning and literacy for decades, and Miss Goode is a well-respected local leader. She remains committed to maintaining the valuable small-town library at its historic location and is willing to sign a new lease, but the terms must be renegotiated. We are preparing a list of minimum necessary repairs and available local inspectors and contractors you may consider. I propose a teleconference in five days to discuss our concerns and can have my people send an invite based upon your availability."

I'm practically breathless. The words ricochet in my mind. *That is untenable. Epicenter for learning and literacy. Well-respected local leader. Valuable small-town library. Public safety. Compliance. Commitment. Minimum necessary repairs. Discuss our concerns.*

He doesn't even offer to pay for the repairs. It's completely understood in his monologue and from the responses he gets from the COO that the company is responsible. I'm stunned and more than a little turned on.

Rom secures an agreement to the meeting and personal contact details of several other corporate executives. He did this within twenty minutes on the phone, stranded on the top of a mountain with three bars of cell service on the day before a major holiday.

I know my jaw must be on the ground as he pockets his phone and pulls me up.

"Let's get you back to the cabin." He rubs my shoulders down to my arms and squeezes my mitten-covered hands. "You look frozen solid."

I blink fast, feeling the weight of little icy bits on my lashes, but the cold? No. I'm burning up inside.

"You're incredible." My breath makes a puffy cloud in the frigid temperature.

"*You're* incredible. It's important that people know that." With his arm around my shoulder, he leads me back down the path to the cabin. "That company needed a wake-up call. Did you hear him mention looking into a corporate-level audit of properties for historic status?"

"I don't even know what that means," I chuckle as I nestle closer into his side. Maybe this is why he always liked books with mystery and plot twists so much. He analyzes and finds ways around an issue I never could, understanding how the parts make up the total. I read books like I read people, for the emotions, the way they move through life, their loves and losses. I always assume the best in people, but has it led me to being too much of a pushover? Rom doesn't see the worst exactly, but he does see boundaries and mechanics I just don't.

"It's a good thing," he assures me.

"That guy didn't sound upset, at least."

"I think he's grateful we came to him first rather than filed a complaint or worse still, a lawsuit. They could get into major trouble if this is a wider problem with their portfolio. We really did them a favor."

We. Rom and Noelle. *We* never spent time together other than in the library as kids, but now we feel like a team. He's looking at the tree line with a distant gaze, and his arm tightens around me. I wonder if he feels the same, the weight of what we could have been: childhood sweethearts, teenagers making out at the top of a mountain. *We* feel so obvious to me — an inevitable romantic duo — if he stayed.

But he didn't then, and he won't now. He'll be gone in less than two weeks. It's a verifiable fact. He has no ties here. His life is in a big city far away. And I don't date outsiders. But I also know that every guy who broke my heart before was different than Rom.

We are different.

As soon as we're in the entryway, we start shedding layers. Coats come off first, and we hang them side by side on these adorable wooden mushroom shaped wall hooks. This place really is so cute with its plant-filled sunroom and old lady aesthetic.

"You're stuck with me for a couple days, at least." He looks at me while tugging off a boot. His glasses fog up in the warmer temperature. "Sorry about that."

"I'm not! It'll be like a vacation." I shed my long sleeve sweater. "I've never had one of those."

Rom's lip curls in horror. "Never had a vacation?"

"My parents lived paycheck to paycheck." I shrug. "And even now, the library doesn't really close long enough for me to take time off. I can't imagine going on vacation while the town just, what, doesn't have a library?" I fiddle with the waistband of my oversized track pants before tugging them off over my shoes, which are stuck on like glue. I'm left in ratty combat boots, bike shorts, and a thin crop top. It's pretty revealing, the kind of thing I lounge around in at home. My lumps and bumps are on full display, but I'm comfortable in my body. I'd rather clean my outer layers tonight since I have nothing else to wear while I'm here.

He looks me over, pausing on my soft, bare stomach then my cleavage. His eyelids flutter slightly before he shakes his head and refocuses on my face. "You have volunteers. Are they capable?"

"Of course they are, but the library is my resp—"

"Then you're taking this time to relax." He interrupts me, hands on his hips with a stern expression. He's down to bare feet, a thin gray undershirt, and matching thermal pants. Illegal. "Trust your volunteers. Trust that the town won't sink into utter chaos without their head librarian.

You are important, don't get me wrong, but you're allowed to take some time off. You deserve that. Give people the opportunity, the joy even, of helping you for once. On that note, you're not to lift a finger while you're here, got it?"

"Yes, sir." I mock salute, and his eyebrow crooks, red eyes swirling to orange then yellow. Rather than squirm under his sexy gaze, I try to toe off my boots again but goodness gracious, they're on tight. My shoelaces got wet near the hot springs and must have iced over when we hiked through the snow. Rookie mistake. I almost lose my footing and face plant. Rom catches me by the elbows before I fall.

"Sit down," he says in an authoritative voice. It's similar to the one he used when making deals on the phone, and I can't help but obey as he leads me to the loveseat. His firm tone doesn't bother me, not one bit. He kneels in front of me with the same intent expression. His big fingers glow a brighter shade of red as he warms up the laces, unties them, and eases the boot off gently like I'm a princess in a fairytale. "You take care of everyone else, but who takes care of you?"

I swallow. "I guess I should?"

"Hmmph." He unties the second shoe, then takes off both my socks. His palms move up my shins and around to grip my calves. Warm skin on skin. And the heat of his hands is nothing to the fire in his eyes, roiling like a living flame. He's so big and strong, so commanding with others but so gentle with me.

"For the next few days, will you let *me* take care of you?"

Oh dear. I lick my lips and he tracks the movement. Carnal visions fill my mind. Afraid of how breathless I'd sound, I simply nod. We're lost in the tender, heated moment until he squeezes my legs once more then stands.

"Good." He gestures to the hallway. "You clean up first. I'll get some tea started, then we can figure out dinner. Consider this your first vacation."

And it took an avalanche to force the issue. Two whole days with Rom in the cutest little cabin. Maybe more. There's no way I'm not going to jump his bones. It's just inevitable at this point, and he seems determined to play it cool. Be sweet.

I turn on the shower and catalog myself. A hot mess express, all tangled hair and stale sweat. But oddly, I'm not exhausted. Being alone with him and this idea of a vacation must have filled me with a second wind. I stick my hand in the shower stream and jerk it back. Freezing. Upon closer inspection, I notice that it's an instant hot water heater, but none of the lights are on. I flick the overhead light on and off. Electricity seems fine otherwise. Just my luck, it's broken.

A wild idea hits me. The hot springs.

Locals love the scenic, soaking pools that dot the mountain from top to bottom where Teapot Lake is filled with their steamy water. And only locals know how to avoid the more dangerous sections like I almost foolishly hiked down.

Lucky for us, I know a spot within walking distance of this very cabin.

And if I was on vacation in the area, it's the first thing I would do. No time like the present, right? Just because Rom is leaving after the New Year doesn't mean I can't compromise on my no-dating-outsiders rule. I don't want to hold myself back from him anymore. I don't think I could if I tried.

I snatch up a bar of local-made natural soap, wrap a towel around my naked body, and grab a second one for Rom. If I'm stuck with this big, sweet demon for a few days on my first vacation *ever,* and knowing how crazy my life is, probably my last, then I'm going to enjoy it.

Chapter Eleven
Rom

I light the gas burner with a snap of my fingers. A ring of blue and orange fire sparks, and I set the kettle to boil. With the water heating, now it's time to prep the rest. I unpack a few tea blends to consider and grab our teacups from earlier, hand washing them in the sink. One of them has a chip in the lip. It's not sharp either, like it happened a long time ago and Old Ethel kept it around for sentimental reasons. Noelle said it was cute, that it gave the little cup character.

Noelle. I sigh. I just don't know where we stand. Well, I know *where* we stand. We're snowed in on the top of a mountain. I'm secretly ecstatic about the turn of events, but she is less so, which leads me to worry about where we stand . . . otherwise. Are we friends or something more? My palms sweat. I'm a confident demon in business, but with women, not so much.

She kissed me first, and it was the avalanche that had us making out a second time. I mean, we could have died. It was just adrenaline, surely. I set the teacups aside and carefully clean the small mesh infuser.

She doesn't date outsiders. Strike number one. But we're friends. That's different, right? We're stuck together for a few days. I'll take her lead. If all she wants is a friendly companion, I'll be that. She has my stash of books to choose from, and I can introduce her to all my favorite ways to relax and unwind.

I pull down an antique serving tray from the cupboard I saw earlier. My reflection in the kitchen window distracts me, and I grimace. Strike two. Someone as beautiful as Noelle would never have a genuine interest in someone who looks like me.

I pull at the collar and sleeves of my long-sleeve shirt to ensure they aren't revealing any scars. My horn caps look dull too. I remove and polish them until they gleam. Not too shabby. I'd prefer to be in thicker pants but changing into a clean pair means encroaching on Noelle's space while she's undressing.

Down, boy. I practically growl at the half chub I've been sporting since seeing her strip down to some tiny shorts and that thin, belly-baring top. It's impossible not to be affected, not to want to run my hands all over her. The woman is built like a roller coaster, and I want a ride.

My train of thought is not helping the situation, and these thermals aren't hiding shit. Think of unpleasant things. Soggy mail. Lukewarm coffee. Fighting with my idiot brothers.

I pump out a set of pushups until the kettle sings from the stove. Yes. I can refocus on the task at hand: giving Noelle the best natural-disaster-turned-vacation of her life. Starting with a great cup of tea.

I select one of my favorite blends, a smooth Earl Grey from this excellent supplier I use for the coffee shop. It's funny, even though I'm not at work, I can still think about it, and it doesn't stress me out. Compartmentalization is key to a healthy work-life balance. Ever since I was a kid and pressured to excel in all the business classes at our private school I found no real joy in, I learned to focus. Do the work as efficiently as possible, because when it's done, it's done.

The pesky habit others have of taking their work home with them has never been an issue for me. My father is the opposite and gets grumbly with me on my days off when I refuse to work. *Lazy boy*, he'd say. But my mother always said I had *a singular skill for putting in the work where it counts.*

Something pokes my arm, and I jump with a rough snort.

"Eep. Sorry." Noelle giggles beside me. "Water heater's busted."

"Oh!" I gesture to the teakettle on the stove and snap my fingers to showcase a quick flame. "Use this hot water to start. I can heat up some more in a pot. You can get the tub lukewarm at least.”

That’s when I turn and really see her. Noelle is wearing nothing but a mischievous look and a tiny towel. I try but fail to restrain my gaze from falling to the cleavage begging to burst out of its confines. Every breath makes her flesh swell against the rough terrycloth.

What I wouldn’t give to stick a finger right in the center and tug it down, to press my lips to her skin there and trail my tongue lower. Mother Below, imagining those abundant curves on full display makes me wish I could offer to sponge bathe her myself, head to toe. Who needs a water heater when you have a demon with fire at his fingertips? Her voice cuts through the fog of inappropriate thoughts.

“I have a better idea.” Her smile has a sensual tilt. “A hot spring.”

“A hot spring?” I close my hands and fist them at my hips. She holds soap and a couple towels too. “Is that safe?”

“Perfectly. The location isn’t dangerous, I promise. And the soap is all-natural, actually designed for the hot springs.” She places one neatly folded towel on the kitchen counter, then steps slowly backward. “Would you join me?”

One eyebrow crooks up, and before I can answer, she darts to the front door, flings it open, and runs outside.

“Noelle!” I shout.

My focus narrows to a single intention. Chase her down. Find her. Get her back. Heart pounding, I snatch up the towel and race outside.

It's not true dark yet, but with the waning light and rising moon, I can still see well. A flash of fiery hair disappears into the tree line, and I run.

This patch of forest is different, a winter wonderland of shallow snow and tall evergreens. A light flurry drifts around me in slow motion. I expect the same dread to fill me at seeing her run away a second time today, but it doesn't.

Her laughter echoes to the left.

My eyes haze, vision in a half-red tint. My mouth salivates. I focus on one thing — the heat of her body. Demons have an ancient instinct, a predator sense that helped us hunt ages ago. It never quite left us, and I let it guide me now, running toward the sound of her voice and the warm pulsing energy of her body nearby.

"Over here!" Her voice is muffled. There's something else drowning her out. Drawing closer, I realize it's the rush of water. The snow on the ground recedes as the temperature rises.

"Noelle," I growl, warning and pleading all at once.

"Follow the lights." Her voice echoes. She's nearby but not in the open. I sense more heat and find myself in front of an overhang that looks different. Blue-flowering vines tangle over the side of a large rock wall, and that's when I see the first wink of light.

A firefly. We learned about these in elementary school. There's an endangered species native to Mount Winter Bliss that migrates from the mountain down to Teapot Lake each night. The geothermal activity means they flourish in this unique environment year-round. And rather than emitting only a warm yellow glow, these glow in a rainbow of colors. I watch as several lime-green, pink, and purple fireflies twist around each other and out into the dusk.

This is it. *Find her.*

Pushing the vines to the side, I notice the entrance to a cave. The movement sets loose another dozen or more fireflies who make their way out toward the lake.

"Noelle?" My voice echoes just like hers did earlier.

The tunnel is dark, but there's light coming from somewhere close. I hear a soft splash of water followed by a sigh. She's here. Making my way in, my hand traces along the rock. The walls are slick and warm, and the air grows more humid with each step. A cavern opens as I approach.

It's a tall space with a round domed roof and an opening in the ceiling that lets in a few speckled snowflakes. The dusky star-filled night peeks through, but that's not the source of light.

A waterfall flows into a large pool, glowing cyan blue from below. Steamy fog curls up from its surface, and fireflies of every color twinkle and float around the room. Some head down past me and out into the night, while others seem content to dance around the dim cavern in dizzying tendrils of light.

She's here. Every burning instinct in my body points me to the hazy form hidden by twinkling steam. As the air shifts, I see her. My breath stops. Noelle stands in the pool with her back to me, fully nude. The two dimples in her lower back wink just above the waterline. She looks over her shoulder. Her body in movement is a symphony of shapes, not only naked but gleaming wet.

She's otherworldly, all voluptuous curves and gleaming skin and wild red hair that catches the limited light and always, ever since the first time I saw her, reminds me of one thing.

Fire.

Demonkind believe our goddesses have hair of flames and lava. They say redheads are our weakness, but for me, that's not true.

Noelle is my weakness. The first girl I ever loved, maybe the only. How could anyone compare?

She's a primal dream awakening something within me I'm not sure I understand.

"Join me." Steam rises from her arm as she raises it toward me. My mouth waters to taste her. She's the feeling I'm looking for when I escape into books. But she's even more than that because she's real. Her hand waves forward several times. "Come on, silly."

I chuckle, and that breaks the spell, at least a little. My body moves forward. I set my folded towel atop her rumpled one, taking a moment to look down at my clothes — long-sleeve shirt and long thermal pants. They cover all the scars except for my face, and I always swim with a shirt on.

She's turned enough that I can see the outline of one breast. The rosy nipple tips downward, just begging to be sucked. The soap sits nearby. I cough to remind myself this may genuinely be two friends sharing an adrenaline-fueled skinny-dipping adventure. A chance to clean up after a long day. It's her vacation after all.

I step into the pool with my clothes still on. I don't want to get so caught up in old memories and new fantasies and how much the very sight of her ignites so much *want* in me that I lose track of reality. It's easy to delude myself into thinking she feels the same, that this is *more* for her too.

Each step into the piping hot water is bliss. I stretch my arms out and roll my head from shoulder to shoulder, trying to center myself, to stay calm and collected in the face of a naked Noelle. The room is too hot though, stoking a growing arousal deep within me. *This* is where my kind are most at home, as close to the fire as we can get, surrounded by heat, but nothing makes me burn like Noelle — her blazing hair, flushed skin, and pink lips. How I wish I could take off these soggy clothes, and be closer to the heat, closer to *her*.

She grabs my hand and leads me deeper into the pool. "This step is tricky."

When I'm waist deep, she turns and hugs me, laying her cheek against my heart. With her arms around me, I let myself hug her back. She doesn't seem to mind me touching her. Soft and perfect. *Mine*, my heart whispers. My mind kicks in. She's mine while she's trapped here at least. Reality check. Then she'll be pulled away by all her to-dos, and I'll have to board a plane away from her. The thought makes my head hurt, so I brush it away.

"I was going to ask you to meet me at midnight at the Truthfire Festival," Noelle mumbles against my chest, and I can barely hear her over the rushing water. I don't know why she's hiding herself to say it either.

I slide my wet hands up her bare back. My cock grows harder with each inch of her body I touch until I grip her face so she looks at me.

"The one next week?" I ask. Is she worried I would say no? The hounds of Enrama couldn't hold me back. "I'll still be in town. Of course I'll go. We'll get off this mountain, mark my word."

She swallows. "No. The winter we were fourteen. I think . . . I think it was the day your family left town."

That day was years ago, yet the old wound reopens so easily, a slicing chill through the center of my chest.

"I hate that we left like that." I growl, remembering the storm cloud of emotions I lived with for years after my parents unceremoniously pulled us out of school and straight into the car to move a thousand miles away. No warning.

No looking back. There was a *unique business opportunity* they had to jump on and making a deal, making *that* deal, was their priority. The emotional effect on their kids was an unnecessary casualty.

"I had it all planned out." She blinks up at me and her hands move to my chest, plucking at the fabric. Even through the wet cotton, she finds the raised line of my biggest scars, and I will myself not to flinch. "Kids aren't allowed into the midnight ritual, you know, but I was going to see if you'd sneak in with me and since demons can't tell a lie on New Year's Eve, I planned to tell you that I had a crush on you and ask if you liked me too."

Like always, her words flow out in a rush, and I'm left thunderstruck. My heart cracks open, full of warring awe and bitter disappointment. She had a crush on *me*? She was going to tell me! I missed that. Not only was she left alone, I also never got to tell her my truth.

"I loved you," I say.

"Rom." She giggles and hides her face in my chest again, hugging around my back, but I can hear the muffled, "We were just kids, but that's sweet."

I hold her tighter, even though my heart aches. Maybe she didn't feel the same. Even if she had a crush then or some attraction to me now, it's not the same way I feel about her, like this is *it*.

Normally I'm not so bold but call it the safety of darkness or the courage of adulthood or the coming holiday where demons embrace honesty. She deserves to know my truth. At least, what mine was back then, what I never got to tell her.

"You can call it puppy love or whatever, but I wouldn't have said I liked you too. That would've been a lie. It was more than that. You were my first true friend and . . . I loved you, Noelle."

Love. Present tense. I can feel it in my gut, every ancient instinct to protect and treasure and adore. She heats my blood like a wildfire with no hope of containment.

She may not be on the same page as me now, but I have hope. Winning Noelle over will take time and patience and a *singular skill for putting in the work where it counts.*

Lucky for us, I have plenty of that.

"You're my dream girl." I make her look up. Those golden honey eyes undo me. "That's what I would have told you then. You still are."

"And we'd have kissed?" she asks. The past is what she's after, confessions of teenage dreams and first love re-done. I can start there. Her feet shuffle closer, jostling her delicious body against me in micro-movements. Wispy curls stick to her temples. "Humans do that on New Year's Eve, you know."

"I've seen it in a movie or two." My palms coast along her side, testing if she likes me touching her, still not believing this is real and not some fever dream. My thumbs spread out under her breasts and stroke up to feel the exquisite heft of what I'm dying to taste. Her skin, everywhere. "You wanted to kiss me?"

She nods and leans forward to peck at my bottom lip. "I still do."

That's it. I meet her the rest of the way. My mouth is ravenous and insistent, licking at the seam of her lips until she sighs and lets me in. Nothing exists except for her. Everything around and between us is wet and hot and impossibly slick. I want to slow down time, stretch the moment just a bit longer. The shape of this woman in my arms, the feel of her, is like no one else before. Noelle wasn't my first kiss, but I'll be damned if she's not my last.

She pushes me back until my ass thumps down on a smooth rock shelf.

"Off." She sidles up between my legs and pulls at my shirt.

I glance around. It's not as dark as I'd like in here with the bright moonlight streaming in and the fireflies and the glowing water.

"I normally swim with a shirt on."

She tugs. "Off."

"I can change clothes later. It's fine. Cold showers are no problem for me." Lies. All lies. I hate cold showers with a passion.

"But hot baths are better, don't you think?" She grabs my hand and massages up, pushing at the sleeve. "Especially if you have a friend willing to scrub your back. But I can't do much with all these clothes on."

"Oh uhhh you don't need to do that." My mind is screaming at me. *I want you to do that! Please, keep touching me!*

"Fair is fair, Rom." Her eyes have that mischievous look again, intent and determined. "If you want to scratch my back, I get to scratch yours."

Her touching me is one thing. But the chance to touch her — to bathe her and help her relax — is too good of a deal to pass up, and she knows it. "Sneaky woman."

She shrugs. "I want you naked, and I'm prepared to bargain like a demon to get it."

"You want me," I repeat, still struggling to believe it. Every physical imperfection runs through my mind like a list.

"You." She nods and tugs at my shirt, sliding her hand over the round of my stomach, making me shiver despite the heat.

It's only fair that she should see all of me. She bares herself to me, body and soul. Trusts me to take care of her worries for her.

And I'm trying to negotiate staying fully clothed in this magical place? Ridiculous.

I've hidden too long in the back of group photos, under layers of camouflaging clothes, behind all these books and fictional worlds. What if the best moments of my life pass me by because of my inability to deal with my shit?

She deserves better than that.

Maybe I do too.

I wrestle my damp shirt off and untie my braid, turning my head so the hair falls over the right side of my face and down my chest. The scars there aren't as easy to hide, so I send up a prayer that the shadows do me some favors. I tug off my eyeglasses, which keep fogging up and set them aside. Immediately, the room becomes a blurry dream of bright water, fireflies, and shadows. One blessing of near-sightedness is that only Noelle is in focus, as it should be.

Her hands smooth up my chest and push my hair back over my shoulders, then fall to the waistband of my pants.

"Off." She tugs at the elastic.

My hips lift and soon enough that fabric plops next to the shirt. Her gaze strays down and I fight the urge to cover myself. I'm terrified and incredibly aroused, cold and hot all at once, half in and half out of the water. The pool glows from below, so there's nothing hiding the effect she has on me, how hard she makes me. I don't know what gives me the confidence to do it, but my hand has a mind of its own and goes down to my straining cock, sliding from root to tip, then back down.

Noelle's lips part. Her chest heaves. This is really real. This perfect woman wants me just as I am — scarred, broken, and ugly-as-sin Rom.

Her hands fall to my knees and up my thighs as I trail my knuckles down her cheek, marveling at every unmarked, creamy inch.

"You're so fucking beautiful," I say. Even my fingers are beastly, thick and hairy, where they trail down the front of her neck, along her clavicle and down the round, drooping slope of her breast. "It's unbelievable how pretty you are."

Unbelievable that you want me.

"You're beautiful too." She grabs my hand and kisses the knuckles. Her lips trail up and down the prominent veins.

I close my eyes and try to stop the gut deep discomfort any time someone pays attention to my body. My experience with women is incredibly limited and always in dark rooms with my shirt on. I prefer to focus on my partner and angle my face away, the only way I've ever felt comfortable enough to sink into a moment and let go. But there's no hiding with Noelle, never has been from the moment we first met . . .

"You don't believe me," she says.

"I think you're kind. The most charitable person I've ever met."

"You think I pity you." She seems sad.

My jaw ticks, and I cover my face in my hands. I want to open up, but I can't say what I believe, what I've experienced before. Sometimes affection starts from a kind person with pity. Another outcast who can see beneath the surface. A woman who doesn't mind a casual fling in the dark. For a chance with Noelle, I'd be okay if it started with pity.

"I don't. Not at all." She closes the distance, moving like a siren, a fiery vision of flushed skin, rosy nipples, and kiss-swollen lips. Her breasts sway as she moves. Her palms smooth from my thighs to my hips to my chest. I'm strong, naturally, but I don't work out like crazy, so my body is round and fleshy. She squeezes and admires every inch on her path up, until my chin is in her grip, and she stands between my legs, towering over me.

"You're a beautiful man," she says, like a goddess making a decree, saying something that she wills to be true. "I don't just mean on the inside, which you are, the way you take on my problems as your own and support me. You're beautiful, physically. This scar always reminded me of a wave." Her fingers trace the big one on my face from where it meets my lip to where it disappears into my hairline. Then she starts tracing the bigger ones on my chest. "But seeing them all now, you're more like a mountain, and these are rivers of lava." Every place she touches tingles. "Don't even try to convince me you're not beautiful. I have eyes, and I like what I see. The way your nose slopes and bends, there's not another like it." She straddles me and pushes back my hair again, tucking it over my torn ear. "I don't want you to hide anything."

Every inch of our bodies align, hip to hip, heart to heart, eye to eye. Our lips meet, and I'm lost to her. Clever hands explore every inch of me. Her hungry mouth steals my breath. Tangled sensations shoot through me. Hot and cold. Desire and vulnerability.

"I want you just as you are. You're perfect to me," she says. Her soft stomach rubs against mine, my hard cock bobbing between us. She thumbs my nipples, then rakes the backs of her nails up my throat before looping her arms around my shoulders. "Do you believe me?"

I nod. It's crazy, but I do.

She wants me.

When my palms coast up her sides, she stops the movement, gripping my wrists and bringing my fingers to her lips.

"And don't even get me started on these bad boys." She growls like a kitten. "I almost got caught drooling over your social media account today."

"These dumb hands?" I twist our grip so I can see the back of them. The tendons and veins flex as I move them. "I do get a lot of flirtatious comments on the photos of me holding books." I never took them for more than a joking compliment, but now I huff in amusement.

"Nope." Her glare is adorable as she presses her lips to my knuckles again then drags her tongue over them. "I licked them. They're mine now."

Surprising the shit out of me, she sucks two of my fingers into her hot mouth. My cock kicks in response. When she grinds again, I grasp her breast with my free hand, hefting and teasing around the areola before moving on to the other. Her nipples are so rosy and tight. She watches the movement and hums a happy sigh, even as her tongue dances around my fingers.

"You like these big hands?" I ask. The fact those words are coming out of my mouth would normally shock me, but I believe that she sees me that way.

"Mmhmm." The sound is messy as she looks up at me with an innocent nod.

I pull my fingers free and flatten my palm on her sternum. She watches its slow descent with hooded eyes as I tease both breasts together for a moment. My wet-fingered hand moves south, leaving a gleaming trail of flesh behind. Obscene. Her tummy quivers as I pass over it. "You want me to put them to good use?"

"Yes." She shifts, swiveling forward to urge me closer. "Yes, please."

I growl, my body purring for her in a deep rumble, like some crazed beast sizing up its next meal. My vision turns gold and hazy. I breathe harder imagining all the things I want to do to her, the things she clearly wants to do with me.

"You're gonna ruin me," I say, even though it's her groaning as I sink a finger inside her hot center. My thumb settles over her clit.

She cries out, then struggles to speak through panted breaths. "Good. That's so good."

"We're snowed in together. That makes you my captive."

Her pussy flutters around me, and I slide another finger inside, wanting to feel more of her taking me. Maybe she likes me commanding.

"I get to use this sweet body however I please, don't I?"

"Unngh. Yes, please." Her eyes are closed, but she smiles a little and swivels her hips. "I'm charitable like that. Kind, somebody once said."

A gruff laugh escapes me. "You're perfect."

"*You* are."

My chest squeezes as I kiss the tip of her chin. "I believe you." My lips make their way across her jaw. "And for the next few days, you're all mine. Mine to spoil in every way."

"You're the boss." Her eyes go half-mast. "I'm all yours."

If only it were true. Forever.

I keep moving my fingers inside her. Like the rest of me, they're not small, and her heat, the tightness of her body, surrounds me. I want more. I pull her closer, my other hand tight on her lower back.

My dream girl, the most beautiful woman I've ever seen, is finally in my arms. Teenage Rom would never have believed something like this was even possible. But we aren't teenagers anymore.

With a sigh, she arches back and grips both of my horns in her hands.

"Shit," I curse. Horns are sensitive. We have plenty of nerves, especially at the base, the exact place Noelle's fingers keep squeezing. "Holy Mother that feels good."

I lean forward, trailing my lips under and around her breast before latching onto a nipple, tonguing and nipping at it while she squirms.

Her pussy flutters around me. She's close.

Demons can sense emotions like a taste sometimes, and all at once Noelle's arousal flows through me in burst of syrupy sweetness. I'm blissed out with the desire to get her over the edge. My thumb rocks over her clit harder, back and forth.

Her hips pick up a stuttered tempo on my lap.

"Just like that," I whisper, bringing my hand up to cradle her jaw until her lust-drunk eyes swim at me. I suck on her bottom lip, bite it, wishing she could taste what I taste, smell what I smell, see how she's so close to finally letting go. "Fucking beautiful. You're almost there."

She licks at my mouth, and I sneak my thumb between her lips. Her tongue rolls around it, and she shudders.

"That's right. You're going to come for me, aren't you?"

She mewls and closes her lips to suck my finger then goes off like dynamite, moaning and clenching around my fingers. Her body circles in my lap as the aftershocks work her over.

Stars dance in my vision, a heady satisfaction and fullness washing over me. I grasp the back of her neck and squeeze, pulling fingers from her pussy free to lick them. Her salty, sunshine taste makes me moan. I'm definitely eating her out next time. No question. I need to taste her from the source and make a mess of myself.

I can barely breathe, my body wound tight and as hard as stone. When I open my eyes, she's staring at me, then my hand with a gaze so drugged and soft I could eat her right up.

"You look . . ." She smiles and sneaks a hand between us to palm my cock. ". . . and feel like a monster."

I chuff, feeling completely free to be myself, scars and all. She likes what she sees and has the glow of a satisfied woman hoping for more.

"And you look like you need to be fucked," I say, testing the waters. Demons and humans need fertility assistance to have children together, so the choice of condom is more of a concern over sexual health.

"Yes, please." She rises on her knees and starts to sink down, working herself a little at a time.

"Whoa." Bliss. Choking, slick bliss. I grab her hips and urge her down, a little at a time. "Grind on me, goddess." The word is a low prayer, fits her perfectly.

My goddess.

I guide her in a gentle pace, struggling not to lose it, finally feeling her bare and closer than we've ever been. Closer than I've ever been with anyone.

The pleasure is absolute, every second something new and miraculous. This is where I want to be forever, pressed against her, moving within her. She pants and mewls with each rough slide as we join. The heat builds between us.

One hand cradles her jaw. I just want her eyes on me at all times. My thumb slides over her cheek. She's precious in every way, taking me inside, further each time. Her dark eyes glitter in the dim light, enraptured and full of emotion. For me. She's *mine*.

Her head turns slightly, and she kisses my hand, nipping at the knuckles and down to the fingers I just had in my mouth, the ones I used to bring her pleasure.

"Let me taste," she says.

I slide them into her mouth and feel the connection to her pussy immediately. She rocks down to the hilt in one smooth, clenching glide. So deep.

I groan. "You weren't joking when you said you like my hands, huh?"

"Nnnn," she mouths.

"Dirty girl," I whisper, manipulating her up and down, our bodies sliding and colliding. We're both soft, bigger people, and it's nothing short of decadent the way we fit together. "You like me filling your mouth and this perfect little pussy at the same time."

On a whimper, she sucks my fingers harder and picks up the pace, her ass slapping against my thighs like a metronome.

I won't last long.

She exhales and braces against my chest, looking down between us in awe. When she thumbs over my nipples, the last of my control unravels.

I thrust up in hard, deep strokes. I'm so deep inside, I can't get any closer. Everything goes tight.

She holds on for dear life, her muscles flexing as she keeps pace with my manic need to drag her down harder. Her pussy clenches around me, rhythmic squeezes that make me see stars. The pleasure is too much.

My release rockets out of me like a thousand-year-old dormant volcano, complete with inelegant grunts.

Even as I'm pulsing, I slide my hand between us and play with her clit. Whispered words of praise fall from my lips as I work her over. "Give in, goddess. Beautiful girl. Come again, just like before. Give it to me."

And soon enough, she's thrashing and falling apart in my arms again. She giggles and hides her face in my neck. Where our bodies meet is hot and wet and pulsing in the aftershocks. I don't want to move or change a thing. Just leave me here.

"Wow. That was intense," I mumble, even as I can't stop touching her.

She kisses me softly. "That was perfect."

My hands roam over her luscious body. I want to commit each curve to memory, promise myself I'll adore them all in more detail later.

We still have time. She's stuck with me, and I'm winning her over. There's no way I can walk away from her.

After some down time cuddling, she hops off my lap with a cheeky, "Bath time."

Back in the water, she soaps up her hands and starts washing her hair, but I slip behind her and take over.

"No, ma'am." I kiss and bite her ear. "That's my job. We made a deal. I'm taking care of you."

"Hmmm. We did, huh?" She wiggles her ass against me, and my body thinks it's ready to go again, but my brain knows I need to pace myself. She looks over her shoulder. "I know you're leaving soon, but if we get off this mountain, you'll go to the Truthfire Festival with me?"

The slope of her neck and shoulders is like art. I can't believe I get to touch her. "There are easier ways to get me to confess I have a big old crush on you."

"Like seducing you in a sexy hot spring until you fuck me senseless?"

"That was an effective strategy, to be sure. Very enjoyable. Feel free to try it on me again." I move her hair over one shoulder and work on her back, getting hard again just from tracing down the divot of her spine. "But yes, of course I'll be there."

"When are you leaving?" she asks.

"January 3rd." My family expects me back to run our flagship store and continue with more Western US expansions.

But the thought of getting in that rental car and watching these mountains fade in the rearview feels impossible now.

"Eleven days," she murmurs. Is there a hint of sadness there, or am I imagining things? I finish washing her hair and soaping up her body.

"Rinse," I say.

"Yes, boss." She looks back at me briefly before dunking underwater to clean off.

An excuse to stay in Winter Bliss would be easy. I could wait to see the official opening of Perkatory. I could monitor the store for a few weeks under the new manager. All logical explanations. The operations back home run like clockwork at this point.

But what if Noelle doesn't want me here long-term? Sure, we just rekindled something, but me immediately encroaching on her life is another story. She assumes I'm leaving, and she's okay with it. If her wild holiday fling starts taking up space in the building next door every day, how awkward would that be for her?

She grabs the soap and cleans my shoulders and chest, eyes soft as her hands slide over me.

"I want to make the most of our time together," I say, hedging my bets. "Even after the roads open."

"Me too." She nods and keeps working but says nothing more. Insecurity starts to whisper in my mind. It's not as loud, but it's there.

"I know you have a lot to do for the festival and fundraiser, so listen, no pressure. Truly. I only want to help. If you get sick of me, I'll be gone. You can forget we ever crossed paths again." It would kill me to leave, but I'd do it. At least, I'd try.

She gets a funny look on her face and shakes her head. Before she can distract herself by washing more of me, I pull her chin back to look at me.

"What is it?" I ask.

"Did you ever think of finding me?" she asks, eyes so big and sweet I want to melt. "That's silly to ask, right? We were just kids, and it's not like I was busting down your door. I mean, I asked around, but no one I talked to really knew your family that well."

"I did. When I was seventeen." I trace the line of her jaw to her ear and tuck some hair back. "I saw a redhead on the street that had waves just like yours and went full internet stalker mode. I'd thought about you before so many times, but thanks to my brother stumbling on to porn, none of us were allowed unrestricted computer access until my junior year of high school."

She's biting back a laugh. It may have been overly dramatic of my mother, but in retrospect it's kind of funny. Probably a blessing in disguise too. As a kid, I didn't really know what I was missing. I knew others had phones and personal emails, but it just was what it was.

"So yeah, I tracked you down. It'd only been three years, but you looked so different." She still looks different. I see hints of that girl I fell in love with as a kid, but I know she's her own woman now. "Always pretty, that's never changed, but older. Distant to me, I guess. And anyway, your main photo was with a guy your age." I grimace. "Very cozy."

"Oh my god. My first boyfriend." She rolls her eyes. "Chad."

"What a name," I grouse.

"Be nice. He's alright." She giggles and pets my chest before getting more soap on her hands.

"My search ended there. Maybe I should have still reached out, but it all felt so strange."

"Because you had a crush on me." She waggles her head proudly.

I can't help but smile. "We've covered that."

As she cleans me off, down to the space behind my ears, I grow languid and fill her in on the rest.

"Life has been . . . predictable. I followed my parents' plans to the T. The perfect, high-achieving son. I got comfortable making Perkatory my whole world. The years flew by until one day I realized I was in my late 20s with nothing to show for myself."

"Um, hello." She slaps my flank lightly. "New coffee shop. The business is expanding! You have plenty to be proud of."

"I mean, personally, I guess. Not business." I kind of love how indignant she gets when I flirt with feeling down on myself. "Business has always been easy. Carving out a part of my life that's for me, not my family, is really why I started my bookish social media accounts. I was just bursting to talk about what I was reading. I wanted a place to be me, really myself, a place I could nerd out and live a little, not just pay the bills and please my parents."

"Your literary commentary is so sharp." She stares at me so earnestly while simultaneously fondling my ass. Is this paradise? "So I guess getting involved with a librarian is some secret fantasy, then?"

I chuckle and squeeze her ass in return. "Oh, you know it! Dream girl, I told you."

She hums against my chest, kissing and nibbling at my large pecs-slash-man-boobs in a way no one has ever treated me. It's addictive.

"I could never forget you," she says, circling back to my insecurity-riddled statement from earlier, that we could go our separate ways and she could easily forget me. Her hands slide to my horns, thumbing over the broken one like a worry stone. "The only reason I didn't recognize you that first day was because you hide so much of yourself."

I swallow. After thinking about why I started the bookish account, I can see what she means. I'm getting there, but I have a long way to go. I sink down on the ledge seat to give her easier access to wash my hair.

"I'm working on that," I promise.

Her breasts sway in front of me as she scratches my scalp. Holy Mother, that feels good. My hands have a mind of their own and can't help but massage and play with her large, heavy tits. Perfection.

"No more hiding! I want to see your face. Your body. Everything. Got it?" She uses my horns like handles to drag my attention up. "And no more talk about us forgetting each other."

"Yes ma'am." I'm probably grinning like a fool because I love it when she manhandles me.

"Oh, the southern politeness coming out. Be still my heart." She goes back to washing my hair, and I go back to feeling her up, pleased to see her nipples react immediately. "Well, you've got plenty of time to get comfortable with me. I'm on my first vacation and even if the roads open tomorrow, I'm staying through Christmas."

"Oh, that's right," I mumble against her chest, drunk on the pleasure tingling through my body as she scratches my scalp. "It's that human gift-giving holiday, the one all the books are about."

"Books?" She chuckles.

"The cutesy love stories in small winter towns. I've read one or two."

"You've read holiday romances?" She pulls my head back and stares at me in delighted shock. "Rinse."

I duck under the water and clean all the soap off, coming up to explain. "If it's a trend in the bookish community, I'm a sucker. When something gets popular online, even if it's not in my normal genres, I'll pick it up. I actually packed one in my suitcase. You can read it, if you want."

"You brought a holiday romance in your suitcase?" Her head is cocked to the side with a funny smile.

"Of course. I'm a well-rounded reader." I scoff. "I brought nine books for this trip, and I have my e-reader stuffed with more than any one person could read in a lifetime."

"Then why did you ask for a temporary library card and spend all that money to have me deliver you books?" She pokes my chest playfully because she knows the answer.

I make a comically cringey face.

"Busted!" she bursts out laughing. "Oh my gosh, someone does have a little crush, hmm?"

"You could say that." I gather her in my arms, wanting to soak in this steamy oasis with her just a moment longer. I could say a lot more than that, like leaving Winter Bliss isn't something I want to do, like I'm sure that she's it for me. Business may be something I've mastered but deals of the heart are a different beast altogether.

I need all the time I can get to figure out the best way to woo my pretty librarian in a permanent way.

Chapter Twelve
Noelle

Dec. 24

"Day one of my vacation." I kiss one eyelid then another, and Rom groans. I move onto trailing my finger over his broken horn. It's surprisingly smooth along the jagged edge, like a puzzle piece waiting for its match.

He grumbles, but his sleepy smile tells me he's not annoyed. There's only one bed in this cute little cabin, and every time I tried to fall asleep last night after the hot springs, his big, sexy body distracted me. Let's just say we stayed up pretty late.

"Why are you awake?" His eyes crack open and in one powerful move, he's on top of me. Over 300 pounds of delicious man presses me into the bed like a preserved flower.

Bliss. "It's your vacation. My lazy ass needs to get up and make you some pancakes. But first, I need *my* breakfast."

His lips press to mine softly once before his slow descent. Goosebumps prickle over my exposed flesh as his chaste kisses fall. First to my cheeks and chin then lower to each nipple until he's nuzzling my belly, and sliding down to —

"Oooh," I moan.

His nose drags through the soft red curls of my mound. He groans and presses his face deeper when I grip both of his curling horns. His tongue licks a hot path up and around, circling my clit. The ridged texture of his horns rubs against my skin as they press me open, keeping me spread for him to work.

"Your taste," he growls out between licks, piercing me with his intense gaze. My beautiful demon. The colors swirl like a firestorm, and I melt every time, sticky heat flooding my core. "Sweet as honey. I'll never have enough."

He shakes his head lightly and gets back to work, pushing my knees up and apart to keep me open. His tongue is warm and fat, flattening as it swipes up my opening then curls around my clit. And the heat! I could swear he's getting hotter, making me squirm like crazy. I'm sure his face is a mess, but he doesn't seem to mind, working me over with filthy, smacking sounds. True to his word, he makes a meal of me.

I moan, arching back and circling my hips for friction.

The vibration of his loud groan brings me close to climax in no time at all. He digs in deeper, elbows sliding up the bed, so his forearms brace my legs open as he licks up every last drop. My hands find his. Our fingers interlace. The full contact intimacy makes me feel powerful, like he's holding me, and I'm holding him. Connected completely.

His eyes open, watching me with a half-lidded expression while he sucks my clit, fluttering his tongue in a tempo so perfect, so steady, so mind-melting, my eyes roll back. I arch off the bed with a formless shout, squeezing his hands until my knuckles turn white.

He lifts off — lips dark and shiny — and slips a single finger inside, thumb gently gliding over my clit as I twitch with the aftershocks.

"Mmmmm. Breakfast of champions." He licks his lips with a proud smirk. His chest heaves as he looms over me, naked in the daylight and completely unaware of how glorious he looks. "You ready for some pancakes, goddess?"

I fall back on a sigh and a laugh. He's too much, but that nickname really does it for me. I'm about twelve hours into this vacation and limp as a noodle from food and sex and more food. Anytime I try to help him with something, he throws me down on the closest surface and makes me come until I'm too wrung out to move.

"Yes, please."

I cuddle up in a blanket at the kitchen table and let him do all the work. I have nothing to do except . . . nothing. It's mind boggling. He really won't let me lift a finger.

All this new time to myself gives me time to think. With most of the big to-dos taken care of for the library, new thoughts are emerging. I whisper voice memo after voice memo into my phone. A recipe I wanted to try that I forgot about until I smelled the breakfast sausages he's cooking. An idea for a special event to celebrate the fae spring equinox holiday.

Rom serves up sausage with a huge plate of white chocolate blueberry pancakes. Savory and sweet. He also makes us some fancy lavender lattes that taste like heaven. I eat until I'm stuffed, then he picks me up and situates me on his lap.

We decide to spend the morning reading together in a big armchair near the plants. The natural light is best there, and the fragrance of flowers and wet dirt is practically an aphrodisiac.

My family isn't religious, but growing up, we followed the popular Christmas traditions. One we always loved was to read a story together on Christmas Eve. Most years it was "The Night Before Christmas." But the only winter-adjacent book in this cabin is the holiday romance Rom packed.

We start to read together and since he reads so much faster, it's my job to turn the pages. That's it. The only responsibility he lets me have. And I love it.

The book is some fancy, hardback special edition with pretty silver edges and blue foil accents on the cover. He bought it because it was all the rage on social media, even though he doesn't normally read romance.

Miss Mistletoe is an enjoyable read so far. A beauty queen's car breaks down at a Christmas tree farm and a grumpy lumberjack takes her in until someone can come tow it. Rom keeps stopping to ask the cutest questions.

"That's not a real thing, is it?" His eyebrow crooks in a charming slant as he peers at me over his glasses. The sexy professor look really works for him. Just remembering his bossy tone in the bedroom makes me squirm.

"Hmm?" I'm getting distracted. He's just so cuddly and sexy, who could blame me?

"A Christmas tree farm." He points to the page where the heroine is stumbling through rows of evergreens in high heels. "Humans really grow a tree for years, chop it down to decorate their living room for a few weeks, and just throw it out after?"

"Some do." I nuzzle his temple, skimming my lips up his textured horns. "They smell really nice."

"What a strange business model. It'd take years to build the inventory." He huffs. "And this part where they're standing under mistletoe. That's made up, right? Surely you don't have to kiss anyone you're caught under this random plant with. That's a sexual harassment lawsuit waiting to happen. I need to make sure my human employees aren't putting those up."

"It's not just about the money. Christmas trees are a family tradition, the magic of the holidays." I point to the book. "Add to that, romance is about the *fantasy*. Don't try to make sense of it with all your distracting questions." The worried little furrow between his thick eyebrows is so cute. I rub at it with my thumb. "You're thinking too black and white. I'm sure the tree farms make money. Otherwise, why do it?"

"Hmmph." He squeezes my hip, a thoughtful gaze darting around my face like he's tallying up revised calculations.

"And mistletoe is just a flirty thing. I've never seen anyone take advantage of it." I kiss his forehead, making my way down his scar. I'm kind of obsessed with it now that he lets me get up close and personal. I love mapping the irregular lines all the way to his plush lower lip, halfway jutting out in a mini pout.

"But you have to kiss the person. It's the rule. Even if you don't like them."

I chuckle. "If it was a demon tradition, I'm sure it would be considered a contractual thing or whatever, but that's not how human traditions work. People use it in a cutesy way to surprise their significant other."

He studies me for a beat, his expression softening, erasing all the silly little wrinkles from his line of questioning.

"Would you have brought mistletoe if we snuck into the Truthfire Festival as kids?"

I smile and hide my face in his hair. Admitting my teenage crush and how I wanted him to kiss me back then makes me feel so bashful, even when my confession ended up in some steamy sexy bath times afterward. And then some.

"I don't know if I'd have been *that* bold," I say. "I didn't even know if you liked me."

"I did." He growls, the sound sending a tremor through my whole body. His grip on me tightens then releases, one hand leisurely rolling over my curves from my knees back up to my shoulders. He adores every inch of me, and I can't get enough. His voice pitches lower. "Very much so, as I've said. So if I find some mistletoe, you'll kiss me?"

"I'll think about it," I tease.

He tickles me, and I squirm on his lap.

"Okay fine!" I say between breathless laughs. "The truth comes out. You can kiss me anytime, day or night. Mistletoe optional."

His thumb notches at my chin as he gently caresses my jaw. "A deal too good to be true." He sips at my lips slowly and keeps his eyes open, watching me in a way I've never been looked at before, like I'm the best thing in his entire the world. Then he pats the side of my ass. "Back to the book. No more distractions, missy."

I wiggle a little, and delight in feeling his cock rouse beneath me. We'll see about distractions. He's been pouncing on me almost nonstop, fingering or eating me out when I try to help him with chores. I need fewer silly questions and more sexy times. As luck would have it, the sexy scenes come quick in this book.

Rom clears his throat when the characters share a heated glance and flirt with barbed words. Enemies-to-lovers light, I'd call it. Then his body temperature starts to rise, like a living heated blanket all around me. He reads faster than me, so he has a lot of spare time between pages. When the hero talks about how good the heroine smells, Rom's nose trails down my neck. When they share their first kiss, Rom's lips slide across my shoulder in featherlight pecks. When the heroine moves into the lumberjack's lap to watch a holiday movie, Rom squeezes my hip. I roll against him a little, looking back to find his hot gaze already on me.

"Keep reading, goddess," he whispers in a teasing tone. "No distractions."

The movie the characters are watching reminds the heroine of all the times she spent alone during the holidays. She gets in her head about it and tries to move off the lumberjack's lap, but his fingers clasp around her throat to make her look at him. He reminds her she's not alone, and when the clothes start coming off, the dirty talk starts up.

Oh, that's hot.

Rom's big sexy hand comes into view, trailing up my arm. I can't take the teasing any longer.

"Screw it." I throw the book on the side table and grab his wrist, urging it up to my throat. He clasps my jaw instead and turns me to face him, eyes solid gold and sparkling. I lick my lips. "It's my vacation. I should do what I want."

"And what's that?" he smirks because he knows the answer. He just likes to hear me say it.

"You."

Dec. 25

"Vacay day two!" I sneak-attack hug him from behind in the kitchen since he woke up earlier than me today. "It smells amazing in here!"

"It's Christmas." He turns, and the serving tray has eggs and bacon for breakfast but also cookies and hot chocolate, complete with mini marshmallows bobbing at the top of the steamy drinks.

He sets it all on a little tufted side table near the fireplace, and we settle down to eat.

"Now I know I don't have a formal gift in trade for the bookmark you gave me, but I want you to have this." He hands me the holiday romance it took us all day to read yesterday. Normally, a novella that size would be a three-hour read, but we reenacted every sex scene in the book, so it was an all-day affair.

"It's beautiful." I trace the shiny blue designs on the front. "I'll treasure it."

"It's worth around $1,700 online with collectors, so if you need more fundraiser money, it's an option."

My jaw drops. "People pay that? I mean, it was a good story, but what on earth?!"

"Collecting books and reading them are not always the same hobby," he chuckles. "It's a limited-edition convention exclusive that later got picked up for movie rights. Think of it like how people collect baseball cards."

"Wow." I bring the page edges to my nose to sniff them. Old books are best, but this still has its appeal. When he goes home, it'll be all I have of our time together. I hug it to my chest. "That's all well and good, but I'll never sell this. I could be up to my eyeballs in debt, and I'll still have this on my bedside table every night."

"Good memories, huh?" His eyebrow crooks, and I love to see the little hint of confidence.

"The best." I boop his nose.

"Then I guess your fundraiser needs to be a success, huh?" he says.

"That's the idea." I set the book aside and get back to breakfast. The eggs are so fluffy, they practically melt in my mouth.

"So, I know what the fundraiser is for . . ." He pauses to sip his hot chocolate with a careful expression. "But tell me what you're setting up for the Truthfire Festival."

"Oh." I eat my breakfast, moaning around the crunchy bacon. "Okay, well, I was just going to advertise the personalized recommendation and book delivery service. But there's also a lot of tourists in town, so I'm going to set out a big donation jar. I have that room full of extra books, a lot of which I need to offload, so I figured I'd give them away as a thank you for every donation."

Rom sets his fork down slowly and steeples his hands, pointer fingers resting against his lips. "Can I make some suggestions?"

"Shoot!" I dig back into the eggs.

"First, you need minimums."

"Minimums," I parrot with a mouthful of food.

"A minimum donation to receive a thank you book."

I nod. Okay, that kinda makes sense. I mean, I would give them away, but a dollar or two seems reasonable.

"And a minimum donation required for personalized recommendation and delivery. You should price out each of those. Consider the distance of the delivery. Run the numbers and make sure it's worth your time."

A mild panicky feeling flutters in my stomach at the mention of numbers. I've tried pricing stuff like that out before, but my brain instantly shuts off. I wave my fork at him.

"It's always worth my time. And I don't know about a minimum for that. A sliding scale option for deliveries means people can give whatever they can afford. And recommendations are always free. Come on, I'm a librarian."

"Most sliding scales have a minimum." He picks up a piece of bacon and chomps on it.

"They do?"

He nods and his eyebrow crooks. Gah, adorable. "What's your overhead?"

"Overhead?" I sip some of my hot chocolate to hide my grimace.

"How much do you spend to do the deliveries?"

"Nothing." I smile.

He frowns and sets his bacon down. His big sexy hand balls up. One at a time, his fingers unfurl as he counts off. "You spend time. You make fliers. If you're on your moped, that's gas money." His hand waves in a circle before returning to his meal. "It's all part of the cost/benefit. How many dollars, on average, do you raise per hour of work on the deliveries? Make sure to include the time it takes to choose the books per person. Your expertise is valuable."

"Oh, that's so hard to say." I swallow down some more of my drink, delighting in the warmth flooding my chest. I have a salary; who cares about hours? "Probably good, though! The fundraiser just crossed the $1,000 mark."

"*Probably good* isn't a dollar amount, Noelle." He takes off his glasses to clean each lens before sliding them back on. "Take my donations out. I'm an outlier."

"Hmmm." Gosh, he's sexy when he uses that tone, even though I feel like a naughty schoolgirl who's not quite catching on. What was the question? Oh right, how much the fundraiser makes on deliveries before he came to town. I do a quick ballpark estimate. "Not so good. Maybe ummm, maybe five dollars an hour."

He slow blinks at me, a muscle in his jaw ticking.

"But roller skating is good for my health, and I deliver for free to people with mobility issues anyway. It's no trouble. You know, I'm representing the library around town. I kind of think of it like public relations. Be a positive presence in Winter Bliss. Make sure everyone knows about our services and classes. And if they learn about the fundraiser in the meantime, all the better. The donations will come."

He stares at me for a beat after I stop rambling. I hide behind my hot chocolate only now seeing how flimsy my rationale is. If wishes were horses, we'd all be riding. These are tough questions, but ones I *do* need to wrestle with rather than run away from.

"You grew up here," he says gently. "So you know this town is mostly demons, and demons aren't too keen on donations with no minimum. You know what the implicit boundaries of the deal are? No minimum means zero, not even a penny. No minimum means a dollar or two if they're feeling generous."

"The demons in this town are very generous." I prickle, then bite my lip because he saw Miss Ethel give me a lollipop and two dollars a few days ago. Is that really her being generous?

"Everything has a price," he says.

"Well, you're generous." I lean forward and boop his nose.

He captures my wrist and kisses my palm, grip sliding to my fingers, where he turns them and kisses the back of my hand. "I was paying for you."

Oh. My eyelashes flutter. That sounds kind of . . . illicit.

He smirks. "I was paying for your time, busy lady." His thick, sexy fingers play with my delicate ones as he peppers more gentle kisses over my knuckles. "You were worth it and so much more. You're priceless." He interlaces our fingers. "Precious."

I move around the side of the table on my knees and push him down on the fur rug, climbing over him. "You have all my time now."

I shift, and the wavy mess of my hair falls to one side. Backlit by the fire, the strands glow bright orange and gold. His hand lifts and gently brushes over them as he watches the colors, slow-blinking like a fire-blissed demon.

When his gaze drifts to my face, he drags me down, kissing me slow and deep until I'm writhing on his lap. Before

I can pull down his sweatpants and give him a Christmas gift of my own, he grips me by the rib cage and heaves me straight up his body until I'm spread eagle on his chest.

Surprised, I shake with laughter.

"Pretty." He groans and grabs my breasts, teasing the nipples with his thumbs and licking his lips. "So pretty."

My hips rock back and forth, wishing for friction, as I grip his meaty forearms.

"This human holiday has its charms," Rom says, nipping at the flesh through the oversized shirt I'm borrowing from him. "I have another present ready to go, if you're game."

His hands slide down to spread my legs open more before shifting to my ass to urge me up to my knees and closer to his mouth.

"Oh." My hands find his horns, grasping for stability.

"Sit on my face, goddess." The colors in his eyes swirl like a firestorm. "And hold on tight."

Dec. 26

"Day three of my vacation is off to a good start!" I smack Rom's butt as we hike down from Frostwing Lookout. The snow gives a satisfying crunch beneath my boots. I love the cozy warmth of our cabin, but there's something invigorating about a sunny winter day.

We had a productive morning on our phones and now have the rest of the day off. Winter Bliss is an apt name these days! I chatted with my two student workers for a good long while. Now that stores are opening after Christmas, they're going shopping and will let me know what supplies they're able to get. We can probably pay for two-day shipping on anything else we need.

I also called the park ranger station, but no one answered, so I left a voicemail for Chad, an ancient history ex-boyfriend. He usually leads search and rescue operations for park services and has lots of buddies that work for the city. I thought he might know something about when the road will be cleared.

Rom only checked his emails, but he doesn't seem upset as we make our way down the hill.

"You have a meeting scheduled with the landlord?" I ask.

He nods. "In two days. I'll take the call up here if I have to but—"

"If the roads clear, you should come down to Winter Bliss and stay with me."

"I'd love that." He smiles down at me. "As for your landlord, all signs point to a positive response based on the communication my lawyer and I received. If not, it's war."

"You sound much too happy about that!" I interlace our fingers. I regret not bringing gloves, but his hands do a much better job warming me up than gloves ever could.

"I want you to own that building, Noelle." He looks down briefly, squeezing my hand, before focusing back on the path. "If you'd let me, I'd offer to negotiate a purchase from them and set you up with some real estate contacts to get a good deal on a mortgage you can afford."

"Whoa. I can barely make rent. That's something I've never even considered."

"You're not ready." He looks back at me, and I can see it's a statement not a question. "Yet. But one day you will be, and I want you to think about it now. To dream big, Noelle, whatever that is. Even if it's not that old building."

It's you, I want to say. My biggest dream would be him living in Winter Bliss with me. He dreams about business, but I dream about people. And I want him. The crazy thought must be some intoxicating mix of happy hormones and the magic of the holidays talking. It's only been a few days.

"I'll think about it," I say.

We just reconnected. He's only passing through. Rom left before, and his family made something of themselves. Winter Bliss is in his rearview, and I need to remember that.

"I was serious about asking my friend to interface with your library's catalog and generate a price sheet of valuable books on hand. She could run the numbers like that." He snaps his fingers and a flame lights up. "Whoops. Sorry.

I'm a little excited about it. But I know that one historical romance Old Ethel has alone is worth some cash."

"Hmmm, that makes me think maybe I could do a raffle at the festival too, especially if I have a book that's really valuable, you know?"

He looks down at me with raised eyebrows, like he knows I know the answer.

I smack his arm. "I'm not giving up *Miss Mistletoe*. No way! Never. It's *my precious*." I hiss at him until he's laughing. "There are plenty others I can bear to part with, I promise. The plan has always been to downsize, even before you rented the place I planned to move into."

"I wish I could say sorry, but I'm not."

"I know, I know." I wave. "Demons are good at making deals, and it's your family business. I totally get it."

"No, you don't. I'm not sorry because it was good for business or because a deal is a deal and too bad for you. I'm not sorry because you shouldn't have to move at all. The library is exactly where it's meant to be." After a few steps, he stops in his tracks. "Wait."

"What?"

"What if I donate a Perkatory Pass? Donors can bid on a chance to win one free specialty drink per day for a whole year. That'd be worth . . ." His eyes dart around. "$1,800 give or take. A little less if people don't go every day." He scratches his chin. "I'll throw in a baked good too and offer one free catering order of up to $600. That's at least a $3,500 value. You could sell a lot of tickets for a raffle like that."

I step back a couple paces. A $3,500 value donation? "That's too much."

"It's not enough." He shakes his head and sets his fists at his hips, looking distinguished and so put together it makes me want to scream. "Plus, I'm not completely altruistic. It'll be good marketing for Winter Bliss's newest coffee shop. You'd be doing me a favor, really."

"Doing you a favor?" I pick up snow, form it into a ball, and hurl it at him.

He gasps in shock, but his face lights up in a way I haven't seen since he was fourteen years old. "What was that for?"

"You need to stop throwing money at me." I lob another snowball at him. "Or I'll keep throwing these at you." I grab another and smack him dead in the face before racing back to the cabin.

"You're in for it now, missy," his dark voice booms. My skin prickles with panic and excitement. I get pelted with a couple snowballs, but I think my roller skating really has done me wonders athletically because he hasn't caught me—

Oof. I land face first in several feet of snow and scramble to turn around.

Right side up, he pins both my hands together with one of his big paws and dusts the snow off my face with the other. His palm is overwarm, probably using some of that fire magic demons make such good use of. Against the bright morning sky, he's a dark god, and I'm struck a little senseless.

"I have another proposition for you," he says.

Yes. My heart calls out, pulse pounding as my mind spins a very specific fantasy.

He plans to throw away his whole life and move to rural Idaho. He wants to be with me for real. He's going to tell me he'll stay.

"No more throwing money at me," I tease, hoping against hope.

"A long-term partnership." He smiles, and I smile back, my heart soaring. "Between Perkatory and the library."

"Huh?" I flash cold like the ground below me and wiggle out from under him, sitting up then quickly moving to stand. I need space to clear my head. That went the completely opposite direction from my delusional thoughts. I dust myself off. "What do you mean?"

Rom has his phone out and is taking notes, glancing up at me with a hopeful smile that kind of kills me. "So even after the festival and you sell some used books, you'll probably still have a lot of inventory, right? Low-priced books but also valuable older stock you can sell to make some cash. What if my coffee shop sells them for you? A partnership where 100% of the profits go back to the library. Perkatory doesn't need a cut. This is just a slight tweak to our business model since our other coffee shops already run free lending libraries. I'd actually feel a little guilty setting up a free lending library right next to your real library."

That would be . . . really cool, actually. Books and coffee go together as naturally as me and Rom. I shake the thought from my head. Gah. Such a hopeless romantic. This demon is too good to be true. "Let me guess. I'd be doing you a favor?"

"Your words, not mine." He holds out his hands.

"You seriously give away free books in all your coffee shops?" I've seen the little lending libraries people set up in their front yards and a couple places that have a bookshelf or two and have always loved the idea. It's pure chaotic goodness. "Doesn't seem very good for business."

"My parents agree with you." He nods with that same cute boyish smile, fidgeting with his hair and pulling it over his right shoulder. "We even have secret rooms hidden behind certain bookcases, if people know how to open them."

I gasp in delight, my fingers covering my lips. "No! Just like in that book we read—"

"—when we were kids," we say together, and he chuckles. "Ha! Yeah, I guess it was my way to keep the wonder and magic of the Winter Bliss library with me. I want everyone to have the chance to read a book no matter what. Just pick one up and go. My time hiding away in your library as a kid changed my life, Noelle. Everyone should have the freedom to read."

My throat feels funny, constricted with emotion. I'm bursting with pride for him and all he's accomplished as well as pride for my uncle and myself. Our small-town library meant something to him. It means something to everyone in Winter Bliss every day. Even if he can't live here with me, the work I do is important.

"You like the idea? Selling your books there?" He seems nervous. "I'll have my lawyer draft up a contract, plain language, nothing funny, and you don't even have to talk to me about it. Make your decision on your own ti—"

"Yes! Of course." I rush forward and hug him. "It's smart, just like you. You've got all the business smarts."

"You've got all the heart." He cups my face with one hand while the other lays across my chest. "The more important of the two."

My heart kicks into overdrive. We would work so well together, personally and professionally. In every possible way. Does he feel it too? Why does someone so perfect for me have to live so far away?

"When we get off this mountain, you can help me pick out some bookshelves for Perkatory and figure out the branding."

"Yes!" I know how busy I can get, but for his last few days here, I'm going to slow down and make time to spend them with him. I'll be home at a reasonable hour, no matter how frantic I get setting up for the festival, especially if we can keep having adult sleepovers at my apartment.

"We have to think of a name for it," he says.

"Second Chance Stories," I say, waggling my eyebrows. "Get it? Purgatory. Old books that need a new life."

"I like it." He leans down and kisses me. "Every story deserves a second chance."

Just like us.

Dec. 27

"Day four," I whisper, leaning over Rom in bed, tracing the angled shape of his eyebrows, then down one of my favorite of his branching scars. I just love to touch him. The sunlight is blue-tinged, barely breaking over the snowy mountain top, but my mind is already in overdrive. It's not four days of vacation I'm thinking about now; it's the seven days I have left until Rom leaves. It feels more real now with each passing day. He's going to leave. The hours are slipping through my fingers like sand.

He ran into someone else on a hike for firewood yesterday, another human woman who got snowed in at a cabin nearby. I *really* want to check my messages. I've been playing phone tag with Chad. His last voicemail confirmed that there are a few of us stranded up here, but he said he can't get search and rescue approved if no one is in immediate danger. The problem is, apparently, we all have shelter, water, electricity, and food. So, no rescue. But he also said he wanted me to call him back. He has another solution in the works, but he didn't say what or when, and I couldn't get through. It's only a handful of days until the New Year's Eve festival, my last big chance for the fundraiser to save the library.

I *need* to get back to Winter Bliss.

"You're worried, goddess." Rom tucks some of my messy morning hair behind my ear and guides my mouth to his for a quick peck before patting my ass. "Let's take a hike. Make some calls. We've got some things to take care of to get your head clear again, huh?"

I nod, heart warming at his continual use of *we*, even though I know the word has a timer on it. Seven days and counting down. "If the roads clear today, you'll come to town and stay with me?"

"Of course. I'm sure the cell service is better down there for my call tomorrow."

And I have the fundraiser. My volunteers can focus on getting supplies while I organize the used books for sale and start selling raffle tickets.

If Rom and I can get off this mountain soon, a couple days is plenty. The number that really haunts me is seven. I only have seven days left with the demon who can sense what I need before I do, the man who takes care of me so well, it inspires me to take better care of myself. I don't know what I'll do without him when he leaves, but I know he'll leave me better off in so many ways.

Old Noelle would kick herself for falling so hard and so fast for someone from out of town. But I can't. Every moment with him has been a treasure. I've never been more grateful I got snowed in on the top of Mount Winter Bliss. These last few days have been worth it and then some. All I can focus on right now is every day, every moment, we have left.

I give him my sunniest smile and nod. "Let's take a hike."

Chapter Thirteen
Rom

*F*ucking Chad.

Listening to Noelle laugh, watching her smile at this guy on the phone sends a hot streak of jealousy through me. On the hike up, she mentioned how her ex-boyfriend from high school is a team lead for local search and rescue. Which is not a job, by the way. I looked it up. It's a volunteer position. His real job is a part-time park ranger. Not impressed.

What kind of name is Chad anyway? How does he expect to be taken seriously with a name like that?

My emails were quick. Everything is set up for my meeting with her landlord tomorrow. I asked my friend to chat tomorrow about scanning the library's inventory for valuable book stock and shot off a quick request for my lawyer to draft up a partnership agreement on our Second Chance Stories concept.

Selling used books through Perkatory should be easy to incorporate if I program the point-of-sale system to log the proceeds into a separate accounting string and set up a monthly reconciliation and payment issuance through my financial team. We've done donation drives before, so I can model it off that process.

"How's your mother doing?" Noelle asks, then laughs at something Chad says. Her cheeks are flushed like two rosy apples. She's so fucking beautiful, it makes me want to take a picture, something to remember when she was all mine. Because if this phone call reminds me of anything, it's that she's about to be everything to that whole damn town again as soon as we get off this mountain.

I can give her space. I will.

But I also plan to offer her help at every opportunity. She accepted my donation of a Perkatory Pass as the raffle prize. That's something we can bump our heads together on as well as getting an inventory check of her library through the system to search for valuable vintage books she can sell. Then setting up Second Chance Stories. I have plenty of reasons to hang around in a professional capacity.

Personally? I'm at war with myself. All signs point to her liking me. Like really liking me. Every time I casually bring up the next few days when we'll be in town together, she's receptive to me spending time with her. She's the one who offered for me to stay with her, after all.

Still, unease tightens my chest.

The next few days will be a way to test how she interacts with me day to day, with everyone else around, her family, library patrons, Old Ethel. *Fucking Chad.* Will I be her friend staying from out of town that she avoids holding hands with? Or will she make it clear that we're romantically linked?

Because we are. We have to be. This isn't casual. There's no way.

"That's really sweet, Chad. You have such a good heart."

My jaw ticks. I don't even know what this guy looks like, but I imagine her with him, anyone other than me, and my whole body lights up with rage. *Mine*, the territorial, demon side of me wants to roar out.

But Noelle is completely genuine. She smiles with her whole face. She's not placating this guy. She's genuinely the nicest fucking person, and I hate that it makes me so nervous. Makes me feel like a monster for wishing she was a little less warm to everyone. Makes me worry that getting together with me was a bit of a charity case. She said it wasn't. She never made me feel less than as a kid either, but damn. A lifetime of feeling unattractive has left me with self-doubt that can turn dark and ugly on a dime.

"One hour. Got it. We'll be ready!" Her smile falters as fucking Chad says something I wish I could hear. "Oh yeah, it's me and my friend who rented Miss Ethel's cabin."

Friend. My chest tightens. *Take a breath,* I remind myself. I have to prepare for the possibility that this was just a casual holiday fling for Noelle. She doesn't date outsiders, after all.

Do I take that flight home next week and ask for a long-distance . . . friendship? I have enough confidence to know she'd want to stay in contact, at least. If so, I could be patient for more. There are all kinds of reasons for me to travel back to Winter Bliss for Perkatory. The manager needs a vacation? I'll put a bug in her ear to encourage it and make sure I'm the first person she calls.

I nod to myself. That's the plan. If things cool down between us when we get to town, if I'm just her friend again, it's not the end of the world. Expect the worst and be happy with scraps. That's the de facto strategy that's kept my head above water so far.

"Mhmm. Thanks so much. I really appreciate it." Noelle tucks her phone away and gives me a thumbs up, but her eyes look a little sad. "He borrowed a vehicle that can make it up the mountain. They've only got it for a few hours, so he said to be ready. They'll be here in one hour."

"What's wrong with that?" I ask.

"It's silly." She shakes her head. "I feel kinda sad to be leaving the cabin so soon."

"I wish we had more time too." I band my arm around her shoulders as we hike back down to the four walls that became our whole world these last few days.

Packing up my stuff takes no time at all. It's just books and a few changes of clothes. When I drag my suitcase to the front door, Noelle is in the kitchen cleaning the last of the dishes.

She shuts off the faucet and wipes her hands dry, smiling at me over her shoulder. The morning sunlight glows around her, and I'm struck at once by a burning bright memory. She looks just like the first time I saw her in that picture window when we were kids, her red hair a messy, glowing halo of light. The prettiest girl I'd ever seen.

"I was going to clean up." I pluck the dishtowel up and hang it on the little mushroom peg above the sink. "It's still your vacation, and you know what that means."

She giggles and rocks her luscious ass against me. "My punishment."

Time isn't on our side anymore. It's slipping away. Too fast. I only have moments left where she's all mine.

I roll her leggings down to just above her knees, pressing her against the counter. One arm stays in front of her, so she's cushioned. This gives me access to her clit as I slide my fingers up and down.

"Spread your legs for me, goddess."

She mewls as she tries to shuffle open as wide as she can within the constraint of her clothes. It's not far enough.

I'm feverish and desperate, falling to my haunches to tear them further down until they're at her ankles and the waistband has popped a few seams. Fuck it. I'll buy her new ones later.

"I need a taste." I brace both palms on her generous ass cheeks and at the same time, she tips her hips to give me access. Spreading her open, I lick a quick stripe from her clit to her hole. "That's it. Let me worship you."

She squeaks and trembles, ending on a high moan as I leisurely lick up and down, toying with her clit. A noisy Noelle is music to my ears, and I eat her like a starved man. Her salty honey taste was made for me. Nothing tastes better than her pleasure.

I dig deeper in, wanting more, not content until she's dripping for me. I know the heat of my tongue sets off her arousal. I can taste it, like the sweetest treat in the world. Soon enough, she's keening, early pulses of her impending orgasm teasing as my thick tongue works inside her at a steady pace.

She's ready, but I want her last orgasm in this cabin to be with me buried inside her.

And we're running out of time.

"So responsive." I stand and whisper in her ear as I make quick work of my zipper, already rock hard. Her eagerness, her sounds, her *everything* makes me so hot; it's like I turn into an animal, something *else* that only has the clearest of goals.

Fuck her and please her.

"You're desperate for this, aren't you?" My cock slides between her thighs, working her swollen pussy lips back and forth. She likes my *boss* voice, as she calls it. "Look how wet I make you. I think you'll miss being my pretty little pet, hmm? All mine."

Tell me you'll miss me, I scream on the inside.

She shakes her head. "You're staying with me until you leave."

I'm staying as long as I can, as long as she'll have me. Mother Below, I can't waste a second more and tilt her hips back, lining the blunt head of my cock up. Her toes scramble off the ground as I hold her in position. Her hands reach up and back, grabbing both horns for leverage as I tease inside, taking it slow.

"I'm right where I belong." Everything fuzzes for a moment as I press in. The feel of her choking the tip of my cock makes me light-headed, but I have to focus. There's something I need from her now. Reassurance. More of her for the little time we have left. "Does that mean I get to keep spoiling you?"

"Unnngh, yes." She's like a doll in my arms, arched back, wet, and ready. Her grip on my horns tightens as she promises, "I'll be home every night."

Home. With her. The yearning that flares to life in me is almost painful. She's making space for me in her life, even if it's only for a few more days. It takes everything in me to not lose control and pound her straight into the counter like an animal. But this is my chance. A final negotiation of our last hours together.

"What time will you be home?" My teeth score her neck as my cock works inside.

"Seven." She wiggles back with little gasps.

"Five." I growl, feeling her clench against me when I bottom out. Her body is a lush paradise, curves everywhere, molded just for my greedy grip.

"Six," she says after a sharp inhale.

"Deal." I toy with her slippery, swollen clit a little more, and the tightness I feel every time I work my way inside her fades.

"Yes." She melts in my arms, our connection silky. Unreal. "Mmmm you feel so good. So hot."

Demons overheat when our emotions heighten and senses sharpen. All that remains is a primal hunger. Her blood sings for me. I can smell it; a tinge of copper in the air, wet earth and golden amber. I can feel it; the spark in my veins, how she's changing me from the inside out, how I'll never be complete without her.

There's nothing I want more than to claim every part of her so no other man, no fucking Chad, ever thinks he can know her like this. I brace an arm up her sternum to hold her throat.

"You're mine." I command as I fuck her, like the force of my feelings makes it true, the submission of my entire spirit. My body and soul. "Take it."

Our reflection in the window isn't clear. It's messy and muddled, but it's perfect. Her arms bent back to grip my horns, my wreck of a face nuzzling up and down her neck. Her tits heaving as I move inside her, steady and deep.

The bouquet of her arousal is so thick; it makes my head spin. Need flares, shooting down my spine to pool at the center of my hips. My cock is the instrument, but everything I am is alive for her.

I slide my cheek against hers, only realizing once I see us in the window that it's the right side, my scarred side, pressed against her perfect flushed skin. Our panting breaths fog the reflection slightly, but it's still us, side by side, as close as can be.

"Perfect," she says, her voice vibrating against my grip. "You're perfect. Never stop."

The rightness of us, skin to skin, breathing in time, moving together as one, undoes me.

"Fuck." I squeeze her tight, her jaw arches up, and I come with a grunt. My fingers work her clit with insistence until she shakes and falls apart for me shortly after. My exhales are stuttered, overcome with an intensity I've never felt before.

I can't lose her.

Even if I leave in a few days, it won't be for long.

She swivels and presses a sweet kiss to my ruined cheek.

A loud honk from outside startles us both.

We fumble to dress, cursing and laughing, and are out the door in under a minute. My emotions are still a tangled mess. I just want to get back to her place and get my head on straight. Find our new normal for the next week. Figure out how to ask for more from her, for everything.

"Chad!" Noelle waves to a wiry-limbed human hanging out the driver's side of a giant, yellow snowcat. It's plain as day in his roving eyes and careful smile. He definitely still has a thing for her.

I lug my suitcase down the snowy steps when he sees me and shakes his head. "Only room for one."

"What?" Noelle looks between him and me with wide, shocked eyes.

I see another park ranger in the front and a massive engine wheel between the first two bucket seats. No room up there and only a small bench seat in the back. A well-dressed demon and small human woman take up most of that space.

That crafty little shit, Chad, did this on purpose. I just know it. Did they really need two fucking rangers to drive this thing? I know for a fact Noelle told him I'd be coming too.

"I can sit on his lap," Noelle offers. It's a sweet thought, but I'm a very big dude, and that's a tight fit as is.

Chad shakes his head with a forced grimace. "One person. Safety first."

I leave my suitcase in the snow and stride forward, holding her hands in mine, heating them up while I lower my voice for privacy. "Listen. I'll stay here. You've got more important things to sort out." Her hair is messy, probably from rutting her like a feral caveman, so I smooth down the wavy tendrils dancing in the winter wind. "I can take my call tomorrow at Frostwing Lookout just fine."

Her nostrils flare, eyes wet, but she nods and leans forward for a kiss. Just like that, in front of everyone and without a thought, she kissed me. I peck her back, still stunned. All my worries about us just being casual, me being a secret, melt away. She really wants me, and I don't want to be the thing she worries about now. She needs reassurance.

"I'm sure it won't take too long for the roads to be cleared," I say, even though I'm not sure. I just can't have her worrying about me when she's already got the weight of the world on her shoulders trying to save the library.

I help hoist her into the vehicle, and she watches me with a dazed, forlorn expression that breaks my heart. After gently closing the door and walking backwards, I get an idea. "Call me!"

She tilts her head, confused. The service up here is shit and calls only get through half the time. Everyone knows that.

"Six o'clock on the dot." I nod to Frostwing Lookout. Hiking half an hour uphill in the snow every night for the chance to talk to her is nothing. I'd do that and so much more. I smile and wink, exuding as much positivity as I can muster despite feeling like I'm about to snap. "A deal is a deal. I'll be waiting."

Her eyes water, but she nods. "A deal is a deal."

That's it. So help me Mother Darkness, I'm getting off this damn mountain if I have to tunnel my way through the avalanche myself. Noelle won't be alone on New Year's Eve ever again.

Chad bangs the side of the massive snow mobile monstrosity, making her jerk and tuck her arms inside the vehicle with one last, tiny wave.

I glare at him, wishing every inconvenient curse upon his head. May his soft bread always come with hard butter. A check engine light with no diagnosis. Milk he doesn't realize is sour until that first lumpy sip.

The engine fires back up, spewing smoke into the clear blue sky, and that dickweed has the gall to salute me.

Fucking Chad.

Chapter Fourteen
Noelle

Oh my gosh, this avalanche really did a number on Mount Winter Bliss. It takes us a full hour to navigate a path to town. I white knuckle it through a long section of crushed trees, clinging to one of my two seatmates, a tiny blonde sweetheart of a woman.

Poor Holly. While I was blissed out, getting spoiled rotten by the sweetest, kindest, sexiest demon in the world, my neighbor in a nearby cabin wasn't doing so hot.

"There, there." I try to offer comfort as another sob racks her body.

"Why would he do that?" she whispers, more to herself than me.

"Men are idiots sometimes," I rub her shoulder, knowing nothing about her situation, but facts are facts. It seems to help as she nods and really starts to let loose, telling me all about this giant demon she accidentally got snowed in with. When I ask his name, I realize it's Az. I only know him casually and while he is very gruff, I always took him for a good guy. Turns out, it was actually Holly that Rom ran into in the woods yesterday. Hearing how he talked up my fundraiser and made a good impression on her leaves me with a bittersweet ache in my heart.

But rather than the chipper woman Rom mentioned meeting, today Holly is a weepy, doe-eyed mess in clothes at least five sizes too large and rather threadbare. I offer to let her borrow some of mine when we get into town and instantly feel better when she accepts.

It's not that I thrive on others' misfortunes, but when I want to keep my mind off my own, it's a real good distraction.

"Hmmph." My other neighbor in the back seat, a tall, elegant demon, makes a huffy sound as he tries to scoot away from me.

"Sorry," I apologize for the third time in ten minutes. It's the polite thing to say even though I can't really help that the space is small. I'm a bigger girl, and the terrain is rough. I shrug my shoulders. "Bumpy, you know?"

Talk about movie star good looks. I don't say anything, but I recognize him as the standoffish demon I bumped into on the sidewalk the first day Rom came into town. His snobbery and fashion sense had me assuming he was a guest at the pricey Emberlight Resort on Mount BZB, so realizing he's been trapped on the rustic and dangerous Mount Winter Bliss is a surprise.

After Holly and I introduce ourselves, he doesn't offer his name. He wiggles over and slumps against the window. I just *know* something is eating at him and try to give him a little grace.

I'm sure they've both been through a lot. And while I'd have thought two tourists would be elated to be saved from this mountain, their miserable demeanors say otherwise. An avalanche followed by a rescue mission in a borrowed, overcrowded snowcat isn't really going to help our vacation-destination image. And well-to-do visitors looking for a cozy winter retreat are what keep this town on the map. It kind of feels like my duty to give them a warm welcome to Winter Bliss.

Holly shudders through another quiet sob.

"Oh no, it'll all be okay." I hug her shoulders and flash the demon a friendly smile, just to let him know I'm here for him when he's ready to talk.

To distract Holly, I jabber away about my fundraiser, which, as expected, works like a charm. She brightens up and immediately hands over a fat stack of cash as a donation, no questions asked. There's got to be at least $1,000 here! Why she's dressed in ratty old clothes yet has multiple stacks of crisp bills is a bit of a mystery. I have a feeling she'll regret throwing money at me once she's thinking straight, but I'll hold onto it for safekeeping. Right now, she needs a friend, and I could use one too.

Holly hands the well-to-do demon my flier, and I brace myself for the worst. It's wrinkled and has a hand-written summary of the raffle idea. I'm not sure how a demon, especially a rich one, will like it.

"How much are tickets?" he asks, reading it carefully.

Oh, this is good.

"It's by donation, so whatever you feel like giving. Choose your price."

"That's a truly terrible idea. You're basically starting negotiations at zero; you realize that, don't you?" His stare goes straight through me.

"What?" I ask. Ugh. This sounds familiar. "No, I'm not."

"You are. You're saying I can pay as little as I want, throw a few cents at you, and I'd be entered to win. You're supposed to start high and give me room for a counteroffer. That's how bargaining works, and you want to strike a good bargain, don't you?"

I blink several times, a little anger building inside me. "That's not really the point."

It's not that I'm dumb, I've just never been out to price gouge people. Rom made the same point, but in a much nicer tone of voice. I sigh, already missing him so much.

"The correct answer is 'yes.' Everyone wants to strike the best bargain possible."

My face flashes hot with annoyance, but before I can snap at him, he lifts his chin and surprises me.

"Now," he says, "tell me you'll sell me a hundred raffle tickets for a thousand dollars."

"But that's so much," I sputter.

"Say it." His eyes flare brighter. A demon making a deal, I know the look.

Holly shoves me in the side and nods encouragingly.

"I'll sell you a hundred tickets for a thousand dollars," I say.

"Five hundred," he says.

Is he serious? This guy has a stone-cold poker face. He should really gamble. Always one to expect the best of people, I smile and lay my hand out, palm up. "Okay!"

"I don't have it on me." He clears his throat, looking a little uncomfortable. "Lost my wallet, but I'm good for it." He heaves a weary sigh before turning back to look out the window.

I think . . . I think he might be serious. Demons don't go around lying about money. I tap the paper in his hand and hope for the best. "The pay app info is on the flier."

He nods solemnly, and Holly and I exchange a wordless, surprised glance.

As we roll past the "Welcome to Winter Bliss" sign, I'm feeling a little more optimistic. There really are generous people out there! I'll sell a bunch of raffle tickets, save the library, and Rom will be down the mountain in no time flat.

Chad and the other park ranger drop us off at the fire station. After a gentle, "No, thank you," to his umpteenth attempt to ask me out on a date and rekindle our ill-fated teenage romance, it's just me, Holly, and the pretty boy demon. He needs a ride back to the resort, and she has nowhere to go. Obviously, that means I'm taking her home with me.

We're three pitiful peas in a pod, so I put on my bravest face and take charge.

Everything happens in a blur. I borrow my uncle's car, and Holly and I dedicate the afternoon to helping our new demon friend sort out a few things. His name is Samite, by the way. We finally got him to crack and open up a little. And boy was I right about there being something eating at him. He's spent the last few days snowed in with Sofia, a local chef with an exacting taste in books. I've got a novel stashed away behind the circulation desk waiting for her right now as a matter of fact. When Samite realizes I know her, he agrees to stay for dinner at my place. Beneath his prickly demeanor, he's just another lost soul who doesn't want to be alone right now. I get it.

By the time I grab my groceries from the library's downstairs fridge and make my way back up to my apartment, my head is spinning. I'm back to my frantic pace of life. *This is my norm.* I've operated at a near-constant, dog-whistle frequency of flurried activity since I can remember.

But today I feel off-kilter. After four days being waited on hand and foot by Rom, learning how to really relax, I can actually *feel* the tightness in my chest and the fuzzy headache simmering behind my eyes.

I'm dehydrated and hungry and all but collapse when I step into my kitchenette and check the time above the stove. 5:50pm. A powerful sigh gusts out. Thank goodness I didn't miss him.

"I need to make a few calls." Samite stands up from my kitchen table, waggling the replacement phone he just got.

"Feel free. We won't listen in." I wink at him and set my things down, grabbing a protein bar and my lemon-infused water from the fridge.

He grimaces. "I'll take a walk. Be back soon." Such a se-cretive guy, that one.

Holly rouses from the couch and rubs her eyes, looking so much better after a change of clothes and power nap. She points at my bathroom. "Can I . . ."

"Please. There are towels if you want a shower. I picked up some groceries. We can have girl dinner. I'm fully stocked with ramen and cheese crackers and fresh figs and rocky road ice cream and half a dozen avocados."

She smiles. "Perfect. I can't thank you enough."

I make a dismissive, messy sound with my lips and wave her off. When the bathroom door clicks, I shuffle to my room and fall face first into my fluffy duvet.

5:58pm. I prop up my phone against a pillow and use its glossy surface to tame down some of my flyaways. I'm sure I look like a hot mess, but I can't bring myself to care. I just want to see Rom again so badly, I'm on the verge of tears. Everything feels so out of control without his steady presence convincing me we've got this all under control. *We.*

At six o'clock on the dot, I dial his number.

His face appears on the screen, pixelated images that flicker and flash in a chaotic dance. The sound of the wind comes across in a scary crackle. His face comes into focus, hair blowing wildly around him and gaze intense.

"Oh my gosh, it's so windy. And a little dark. I don't like that it's so dark and you hiked all the way up th—"

"I'm fine, goddess." He shows me the flashlight in his opposite hand. He's prepared.

I sigh and just take in the sight of him, so glad I made it home in time for this call. While it was super fun going full steam ahead to help Holly and Samite get situated to-day, boundaries are also important. I need to make sure I'm home at a reasonable hour, that I have a balanced meal for dinner. Drink eight glasses of water. Shoot, I may even take up journaling!

And at least for the next week, I have these telephone dates with Rom to get me on self-care training wheels. I'll be home by 6:00pm every night no matter what.

"You're thinking awful loud," Rom says. "Want to tell me what's on your mind?"

For the next hour, we talk about our days. He decided to reread the books I picked out and made it all the way to this really sexy moment two characters share in a bathroom. They're best friends and it's the slowest of slow burns. Mmmm, that scene kills me every time. Soon enough, I'm squirming, wishing Rom was here to hold me.

I insist we end the call because it's so dark, but he compromises that he'll hike back if we keep talking until the reception drops out. Ugh, I don't want him in a snowy wilderness alone. I want him *here*. Seeing that black screen cut him off halfway through his thoughts on the class differences in the story's worldbuilding makes a lump form in my throat.

"6:00pm tomorrow," I whisper to the screen and take a deep, cleansing breath.

Then, it's back to my new friends.

I take a quick shower, and Holly and I throw dinner together. She's a teacher, which makes total sense. Librarians and teachers go together like peaches and cream, so it's no surprise we click as well as we do. She's an absolute sweetheart with the goofiest sense of humor.

Samite should be back any minute now. We giggle over Holly accidentally calling him Sam earlier. His lip curled in the most comical way, and it made us both absolutely crack up. He *hates* it, which just means we call him Sam as a general rule now. He's an easy demon to rile up, but it's all in good fun. And frankly, he deserves some good old-fashioned teasing.

Samite strides through the front door and proceeds to grumble over our offerings while still expecting to eat like a king.

Holly and I lay my dollar-store dish towels over our forearms and flourish each plate before placing it on the coffee table like we're vying for a Michelin star.

"Sun-ripened avocado on a bed of crispy smoked cheddar with a hint of lemon," I say in a sing-song voice for the avocado chunks on cheese crackers. Adding a drop of lemonade on each was Holly's genius idea.

"Delicate noodles softened in a garlic-infused broth over an open flame," Holly introduces the ramen with impeccable delivery.

"And a frozen fig delicacy for dessert." I set three coffee cups filled with the last of my rocky road topped with diced dried figs.

Samite sniffs the avocado cracker and eats it with the grace of a celebrity chef judge.

"This is palatable," he says, both grabby hands already reaching for more.

"Thank you, Sam." I bow and smirk at Holly.

"Sam-I-Am. Would you prefer green eggs and ham?" Holly barely gets the words out before we both dissolve into giggles.

Samite actually cracks a smile, and I know we've finally got him. I pull out the reserves from my closet — leftover Halloween candy — and we all get a little sugar-high as talk turns to our slightly tragic love lives.

I tell them about Rom, and they remind me to trust my gut. Samite shares that he fears his feelings for Sofia may not be reciprocated. We tell him to woo the shit out of her as a last resort. Holly spills more about the hot-and-cold situationship she found herself in with Az. She knows she deserves an apology, and I really hope she gets one.

Samite decides to extend his stay through the New Year's Eve festival, and we make plans for lunch tomorrow. Holly is quite literally stuck in town. Her rental car and all her belongings are buried under the avalanche, so she has to wait in town until they can dig it out. Thankfully, she's in better spirits and seems excited about helping me with the library's fundraiser.

The sun sets, filtering its warm pink light across my messy living room. As of this morning, we were three strangers thrust together by fate and a shared natural disaster. But here we are eating junk food, oversharing, and laughing like we've known each other for years. Friendship has a way of taking you by surprise that way.

By nightfall, Holly, Samite, and I are three much-less pitiful peas in a pod. You might even call us hopeful.

WINTER
BLISS
LIBRARY

Dec. 31

It's New Year's Eve.

Everything is perfect.

Well, almost everything.

It's been *four days*, and Last Hour Road still isn't clear. Everything I'm hearing around town says the road crew made a lot of progress up the mountain but may cut out early today because of the holiday. Since Miss Ethel's cabin is so high up, Rom probably won't be able to get down the mountain until tomorrow.

"We sold out of raffle tickets!" Holly looks up at me with pride from our festive fundraiser table near the town square. She's been such a huge help these last few days, along with Samite, Uncle Darren, and my student workers. Everyone really pitched in when I gave in and finally asked for help.

"$15,000," I whisper in awe, roller skating over to the fundraiser poster and coloring the green up to the top line. Fran and Than are still working the impromptu used book sale table on the other side of the square, so that number may be even higher. All that stress, months of worrying if I'd ever be out from under all the back bills, if I'd ever actually live with a buffer, and just like that . . . "We did it."

A small crowd has gathered to hear the winner of the raffle announced. The generous prize of endless drinks, snacks, and a catering order from the new coffee shop in town has really gotten Perkatory a lot of buzz.

I look over the smiling faces of so many people I recognize, mostly demons since it's their big holiday, but there's a good mix of orc, human, fae, and shifters in this town too. We have such a supportive community, so many kind-hearted people. Times like these make all the hard work of running the library worth it.

"Okay, here we go," I sing out as my arm digs around the large fishbowl full of entries. "The grand prize winner is" — I pull out a ticket — "A835."

"It's me?" A familiar gasp sounds out. "I never win any-thing!"

The flushed face of a library regular steps to the front.

"It couldn't have gone to a more deserving person." I give her a big hug and send up thanks to the powers that be that it was an overworked single mom that won. What a treat that she'll be able to pick up a drink before every nursing shift for the next year.

"Everybody is a winner, though!" I flash a stack of tickets I just printed up this morning. "One free specialty drink of your choice when Perkatory opens next month. Special thanks to the Perchaz family for their generosity." I get a little choked up at that part but keep it together, bolstered by all the hugs and handshakes as folks congratulate us on a successful fundraiser.

$15,000. It still doesn't feel real.

My uncle stands in front of the fundraiser chart, his arm looped through the supervisor from the memory care facility. The two of them have helped us so much over the last few days.

"What's this?" he asks. The lines on his forehead tell me he's probably stuck in a mental fog right now.

"The library is going to get a bunch of upgrades." I paste on a smile even though emotion burns in my throat. I'm simultaneously super proud of what we've accomplished and upset that it had to be when the man who led the library for decades can't fully experience its future.

"A new radiator?" he asks.

I shake my head. He replaced that years ago. "The radiator's doing good. This is for some touch ups. Paint, light fixtures, and some furniture. The fundraiser did so well, we can even bring on a new part-time librarian."

I use *we* just in case he's not clear that I'm in charge now. And there's more I don't say about the fundraiser out loud, because it's too much to get into if he's not in the right frame of mind.

So much I can scarcely believe it's all real.

I just signed a stellar new lease with my landlord; stabilized rent at the same rate I'm paying now for a new five-year agreement. I also get the first right of refusal on a mortgage if they choose to sell the building. All structural repairs will be completed by the end of March on their dime as they work to get everything up to code before the building's first historic property inspection.

My uncle nods and fidgets with his ring, a nervous habit he's always had. He traces the back of his hand with a thumb, eyes flitting over the weathered, thin skin.

He glances up, pausing for a beat to look me over. "Noey?"

I recognize that expression on his face. He's confused and right on the brink of being scared by it. He needs to *know* something for sure, even if that's a someone. I'll never not be that for him. I always want to be his safe place, even if it grows more bittersweet each day.

"It's me. Up to no Goode." I pinch my lips to the side, my vision swimming as I skate over to hug him. They say touch helps people struggling with memory loss, and I've always been a hugger, so it helps me too.

We rock together for a moment before he whispers in my hair, "You're so old."

I chuckle and squeeze him tighter. "So are you, ya old goof."

I wonder for a moment which Noelle he expected to see. The eight-year-old who just learned to skate? The fourteen-year-old with her first heartbreak?

"You're in charge of the library now?" he asks.

I nod and know he can feel it since we're cheek to cheek. I go with a few reassurances that help most of the time.

"You're retired. Happy. You volunteer when you can. The library is doing great." My voice cracks, still processing how true that is. The fundraiser was such a success that the money raised can really go to improvements rather than just staying afloat.

He pulls back, and his eyes dance over my face. Maybe I'm the little kid in a grown woman's body, and he's seeing me again for the first time. I wish I had a way of knowing what this is like for him.

"I'm proud of you." He squeezes my shoulders like he's trying to physically cement our connection. "I've always been proud of you. I hope you know that."

"I know." I hug him again, so he doesn't get alarmed that there are tears falling down my face. For me, crying doesn't only happen when I'm happy or sad. It's a pressure release valve. I cry anytime the emotions get too much to hold in, and today has been a super emotional day.

Saving the library may be a holiday miracle, but some things can't be fixed with a magic wand. Sometimes life takes an irrevocable turn, and we have no choice but to adapt. Find a new normal. Hold tight to all the good we can, whatever we have left.

"A raffle!" He points at the sign, and we break apart. "How smart. That radiator does need repairing."

The supervisor from the facility nods at me and steps up, looping her arm through his.

"Did you know we have a coffee shop now?" He reads the sign and looks at her. "We should check that out."

"We will." She pats his arm. "It hasn't opened up yet, but soon."

I wave as they leave and finish clearing off the table. My phone alarm chimes. 5:50pm pulses on my screen in black and white. Butterflies set off in my stomach.

"I'll go grab some boxes to pack up." I tell Holly, who's already stacking supplies and breaking things down.

"Mmhmm." She waves me off with a knowing smile. At this point, she's well aware of my nightly standing call at 6 o'clock. I love that she's dressed to the nines in a velvet burgundy dress and white shawl. She's really bounced back from when we first met and embraced this little town like it's her own.

"Thanks, girl." I navigate my way through the crowd, slightly taller than most because of my roller skates. The parade is finishing up as the town moves from the family-friendly festival to adults-only party mode.

Fire dancers twirl down Main Street, the ends of their skirts alight as they spin and shift around each other in a dizzying dance. Stilt walkers hand out sparklers to kids. The high school marching band, dressed all in red and orange, fill the streets with a happy tune. Somehow, the tuba's horn bursts out flames with each loud honk.

Nearby, crews of demons are setting up the fire altars along the road and the main square. Soon, the Devout, a religious sect of demonkind, will do their fancy incantation to conjure a lava eruption from Mount Winter Bliss. It helps keep the volcano stable and the townsfolk safe, but mostly I love the whole shebang because come on, half naked demons doing fire magic?

It's pretty stinking cool.

As nightfall approaches, big wigs from all over gather for the prestigious honor of leading a torch-lit procession from city hall to the town square, lighting the altars as they go. Visitors toss in their offerings, usually sentimental objects or notes meant to symbolically bid farewell to the past year. As the New Year's ball drops, the magical ritual begins.

It's almost mythic, one of those moments where being part of this town feels like I'm a part of something bigger than myself.

Tonight, there's only one person I want to experience it with, but he's still snowed in miles away.

There's no way he'll be here.

All the success of the fundraiser, all the joy and hope of the new year surrounding me, none of it can distract me any longer from my aching heart.

I unlock the library's front door and dial Rom's number, wedging the phone between my shoulder and my ear as I grab some boxes and make my way to the front window.

No answer. Hmm. That's odd.

I stare out the stained glass. The window pane is red, and I see Winter Bliss, my whole little world, through truly rose-colored glasses. The holidays are full of so much joy, even when it's bittersweet. Families walk by, bundled up and laughing. A horse-drawn carriage drifts by carrying two lovers. Groups of revelers laugh and dance across the street. A light flurry drifts over the scene of a small town filled with festive lights and the dots of fires just getting started.

Winter Bliss is my home. I can't see myself anywhere else.

But I want Rom too. And I want him here.

I call his number again, and he picks up with a garbled, "Noelle?"

"Is everything okay?" I ask.

"I'm fine." His voice cuts out, but his tone isn't distressed. The line crackles. "See . . . and . . . do . . . urch." Followed by a crystal clear. "Okay?"

"I can't hear you." I clutch the phone; my words slow and overloud like any of that will help when clearly the service isn't great. Maybe the weather is bad up on Frostwing tonight. I didn't even check to see. "Be careful, please. I'll talk to you tomorrow, okay?"

"Were . . . fine . . ." and the line goes dead.

Ugh. So much for our call tonight. It sounded like he said he was fine, at least a couple times. I'm sure it's the weather or local cell phone lines being used a lot since it's a busy holiday. I don't know how any of that works. This just isn't how I saw our last week together going, garbled words over bad connections.

"Three days," I whisper to myself.

It's less time than we had in the cabin together. Each hour is like a death knell in my heart. The fact I'm so glum about it makes me feel guilty. I have my family. I have this town. Most of all, I have my purpose. The library. It just sucks that everyone I hit it off with — Rom, Holly, Samite — seems to only be passing through.

While I stay in Winter Bliss, alone.

Sure, I could try to keep in touch, flirt long-distance with Rom or even settle for stalking his social media and being internet besties. But I know what always happens. We'll play phone tag and slowly fall out of contact. I don't know how much of the heartache I can take. It makes me sympathize with some of the older locals who close themselves off to visitors and only chit chat at arm's length. I get it.

But that's just not me. I love with all that I have, and I like that about me.

"Love." My breath fogs up the glass. I trace a heart with my finger and smile.

He said he loved me back then. It was sweet, and I assumed he just meant a childhood sweetheart kind of thing. But I still feel it now, and I think he does too.

To be with him might mean dealing with a few missed connections, but I can adjust. Even if a long-distance relationship is full of challenges, Rom is worth the extra effort. He's worth everything to me.

I reposition the boxes at my side and open the door, determined to enjoy my New Year's Eve. I may not see him tonight, but tomorrow I'll tell him what I want.

A second chance at first love.

Chapter Fifteen
Rom

"**I** can do this." I crack my neck and stare across the dark surface of Teapot Lake.

Water isn't a demon's favorite thing. We prefer a dry heat, mountains with seismic activity, maybe a beach if there's plenty of sun. It's not that I can't swim. I can. I can swim this lake quite well, in fact.

Well . . . I could. I doggy paddled this distance as a snot-nosed kid more times than I can count, just not in the dark. Alone. Powered by my rather large and slightly out of shape physique. If nothing else, I know I float.

I shake my head and snort, rubbing my temples up to the base of my horns. "I can do this."

I take off my nylon drawstring backpack and set it on the ground. It's stuffed with a change of clothes and some toiletries in several gallon-size plastic bags. I send down a prayer that they're truly as watertight as the packaging implies. Besides the contents of my backpack, the rest of my belongings will stay at the cabin until the roads are clear.

After a five-hour hike, I have to catch my breath. My phone conversation with Noelle was a total shitshow. Hopefully, she at least caught my repeated reassurances that I was fine and that I'd see her tonight, and if I didn't show up to the festival by midnight, she should send search and rescue to the lake. I was joking when I said that part, but watching the sunset fade from sherbet pink to a darker shade of violet, the nerves are setting in.

That's a big ass lake, and true dark is coming quick.

I'd love to jump in and start swimming now, but I've been hiking all day already and feel a little weak. I have a quarter gallon of water left and a decent meal of jerky, nuts, and dried fruit to eat. My body will need all the rest, hydration, and fuel it can get. Plus, when the sun disappears, it's Silent Hour, demonkind's most sacred feast. The last meal before the new year. I'm not really religious or anything, but like most demons, I'm superstitious enough to honor Mother Darkness. You know, just in case. Because it was this day, this night, that she promised when tomorrow comes, each new day would be brighter.

That's all I want. To watch the sun rise tomorrow and tomorrow and tomorrow with my best friend.

I tap my phone, but there's no service here. Figures. The sky is fading to a deeper indigo. I flick on my mini flashlight and start to eat.

It's been a pretty wild day. After hiking to Frostwing Lookout this morning and suffering through the emergency operator's wishy-washy update that the roads should be clear within the next 12-36 hours, I knew there was only one way off this mountain. The same one Noelle almost took days ago. The route that sent me into a panic.

My thoughts are clearer now.

The mountain is a monster and a mother. I just needed to treat her with respect. The first step in that was learning.

The trail map Noelle gave me days ago was goddess-sent. I studied it and ended up choosing the safest route. It also happened to be the longest and furthest from Winter Bliss. No lava pits or magma rivers or bear dens for me, thanks.

It's almost 10:00 pm by the time I've had a meal and run myself through a heaping dose of affirmations. I stand on a rocky overhang. The water is deep here and a straight shot to town. I've done this before.

"I can do this." I tighten the straps of my bag, clicking the buckle across my bare chest. My hand goes to my nose to readjust eyeglasses that aren't there. I switched to contact lenses. Better than losing my $300 custom prescriptions at the bottom of the lake. Thankfully, vacation-minded Rom of two weeks ago also packed swim shorts, thinking he'd find a nice hotel with a pool.

Oh, how differently this trip has turned out. After surviving an avalanche, I'm about to swim alone across a deep, dark lake in the middle of the night. And I wouldn't change a thing.

Light dances across the water's surface from the moon, thousands of multi-colored fireflies, and the twinkling town of Winter Bliss on the opposite shoreline.

Can I really do this?

I imagine Noelle waiting for me at the town square on New Year's Eve, just like she must have fourteen years ago when everything went to shit.

"Fuck it."

I dive in.

The water isn't a shock at all. It feels good. Great, actually, like a hot tub that hasn't quite reached maximum temperature. A nice, warm bath.

I swim for a while and monitor my heartrate as I go. When I get tired, I turn on my back to catch my breath, watching my chest heave. Slow and steady wins the race.

Fireflies flit around me, several landing on my nose and belly, then shoot off in a swirling vortex that dips and flows from the water's surface to the cooler air and back again. They kind of remind me of a flock of starlings, how thousands of them move as if of one mind.

I can't wait to tell Noelle about this, even if she's seen it a hundred times. My childhood memories are pleasant enough, but re-experiencing Winter Bliss as an adult has been so special. Despite the mountain's treacherous inclines and other natural hazards, it really lives up to its name tonight. The terrain is dangerous in a way I understand, its ferocity carved into my skin. The scars are like the rivers of lava themselves. They aren't embarrassing. They remind me I survived. I'm alive. And every time I venture out and face my fears, I'm brave.

Dark water surrounds me in a comforting embrace, warmed by the heat of the very earth below. Darkness is a demon's home. This place is my home, where I'm meant to be.

With that thought in mind, I get back to the task at hand, a brisk freestyle, and keep the glow of the town in front of me. The shoreline isn't just the yellow and blue lights of houses and businesses. The fire altars are being lit near the city hall. Flames and smoke pump into the starlit sky like a signal to the gods.

Excitement builds in my gut. I'm so close I can feel it. The collective energy of some powerful demon fire-magic is beginning. Mount Winter Bliss is about to erupt with controlled lava flows that will keep the mountain, the town, and the entire region safe for another year.

My feet hit the muddy bottom. I made it! The first thing I do is pull out the bag holding my phone.

11:40pm. My legs are like jelly, but I make my way toward the town square by following the streetlights, then the flames. Torches light the way as a dark group of half-naked fire-conjurers march past.

This is cool as shit. I never got to see it as a kid, since only adults could attend the midnight ritual and after party.

Someone hands me a torch and just like that, I'm swept up in the procession of the Devout. Male members of the religious demon sect wear black loincloths while the women don simple two pieces. Everyone is soaking wet from head to toe to repel fire catching on their clothes or hair. I can understand the confusion considering I'm also still wet and wearing small black swim shorts.

A priest-looking guy paints blue symbols all over my body before I can even react. Weird, but okay, because rather than push him away and hand back the torch, I march alongside them. The entire town will be paying attention to the procession. It's the best vantage point to find Noelle. The Devout light each fire altar in our path with their torches, while I search the crowds lining the street.

Redheads stick out, but she's nowhere to be found.

Then, I'm out of time. We've reached the town square.

The Devout dump their torches in a giant bonfire and circle up. Before I can slip away, my neighbors grab my hands. It's a perfect circle of a couple dozen serious, fire-magic demons and me, a random dude in swim briefs.

"And now the time for our truths. Speak now or hold your secrets in silent shame."

It's Old Ethel.

Gobsmacked, I had no idea she was a practitioner of the ancient rites. No one steps forward, but the two hands clasping mine start to heat up. Shit. The magic is starting?

"Jaromar!" Old Ethel's hand sweeps to me. "You have something to share."

I stumble forward, more worried about fucking up the magic than figuring out why she called my name. Her other hand sweeps to the crowd. "Noelle!"

Between two burly young demons, the redheaded beauty I traversed a mountain and swam across a lake and marched through the streets to find steps into the circle. Mother Below, she's beautiful. Just perfect in every way wearing a glittering yellow-gold dress. Her eyes are wide but not afraid. No, she's lost in a state of total wonder. Noelle sees Old Ethel first.

"Me?" She presses a hand to her chest as she moves forward on her roller skates, twirling to glance at the circle of the Devout. "I . . . what . . ."

Our eyes meet. She blinks several times, looking me over from head to toe. Almost . . . confused. Like an out-of-body experience, I see myself through her eyes. I'm in nothing more than the tightest swim shorts with my hair knotted back. In public. Nothing hides my face or my chest, not even my glasses.

I'm tired of hiding.

I stand before her and all of demonkind just as I am, covered in scars with half an ear and a misshapen nose only a mother could love. Well, maybe Noelle too, if I'm lucky. If I'm honest with her first.

We move together like magnets. Old Ethel joins our hands and melds back into the circle.

The Devout begin to whisper, words so quiet I can't make them out, but each demon's mouth is completely in sync. Fireballs circle their joined hands, swirling with unholy light.

"We were chosen." Noelle's eyes dart around. "I don't understand. The people chosen for the conjuring have to share something with each other." She locks eyes with me, silent for a beat before her eyes widen. "A hard truth we're holding secret."

"What if it's not hard?" I ask.

"Mine is." She shifts on her skates. It's nice she's a little taller in them, almost eye level with me now. "I mean, maybe not."

I clasp her hands in mine, hoping my fingers don't burn her from all the chaotic energy zinging around inside me. Her hard truth can't be that bad. It's Noelle. She's pure goodness. She'd never hurt me. I have to be brave and face it, whatever it is.

I have to tell her *my* truth, the one I kept safe in my heart all these years. The one I half confessed to in the cave but held back the hard part because I was scared.

I'm not scared anymore.

I don't want to hide anything from her.

"Let's both say it together." My forehead leans down against hers.

"On the count of three?" She gives me a little smile. Nervous but ready.

"The count of three." I squeeze her hand.

"Three," we say together. The demons shoot fireballs toward the ground.

"Two." Flames catch and race along a pattern that surrounds us.

"One." Intricate shapes alight. It's a blazing sigil. The sight distracts us until it flares in a brief, hot burst.

We lock eyes.

"I love you," we say at the same time, followed by a twin reaction. "Really?"

The fiery lines surrounding us grow tall, dancing like living spirits, and the Devout begin chanting. I grasp her tight on a surprised laugh. We watch from the center of the entire town, enraptured and hypnotized by the ritual. The flames morph from red to orange to yellow to white gold. The demons surrounding us are dark silhouettes, hands held high and ablaze as their multi-layered song echoes through my bones.

I feel light and heavy at the same time. Infinite.

"You love me?" I ask, sneaking a glance back to her. It doesn't seem real.

"And you love me." She pulls my face down and peppers it with kisses.

I can't stop smiling between kissing her back, getting as close as I possibly can until a flash of heat has us and the crowd gasping.

The eyes of every Devout member are white gold and swirling, their hands clasped high. Fire is everywhere, tall and fierce but contained.

Then, the dancing flames seep into the ground. As the firelight recedes, the earth itself begins to glow. Every head swivels to Mount Winter Bliss, a looming monolith against a violet sky. The tip of the mountain erupts in a spray of orange and gold.

Boom!

The crowd cheers in a cacophonous roar. Bright wavy rivers of lava flow down the mountain into channels the first demons to live in this valley dug into the rock ages ago.

Noelle's eyes reflect the bonfires around us and the stars above. This is her town, her mountain, but I want it to be mine again too.

"I want to stay," I say, not even sure she can hear me over all the noise.

She turns, eyebrows up and speechless. Her arms loop around my neck, and she jumps. I catch her easily and we're nose to nose, forehead to forehead.

"I want you to stay," she says. "But are you sure this little town is enough for you? I'm okay with long-distance. I'll do whatev—"

"I'm not okay with *any* distance." I squeeze her tighter, so she's pressed against every inch of my bare chest, and my hand is in her beautiful hair, keeping her face close too. Right where she needs to be. Right where I belong. "You're everything to me. My past *and* my future. There's nowhere else I want to be than with you."

Tears stream down her face, catching the light of a hundred fires. As we kiss and kiss, the exhales of her laughter and salt of her happy tears takes me higher, makes me hungry for more. She's my forever and my right now. I'm so lost in the moment; there's no one else but me and her.

"Oof, sorry." A shirtless demon covered in body paint with streamers tied to his tall horns bumps into me. With the ritual over, the Devout dispersed, and I guess we're standing in the middle of what's now the dance floor. A live band is starting up some drum-heavy folk music.

Noelle seems to know the guy and his companion, and even when I set her down, she keeps a stranglehold hug on my waist. My girl is a sucker for chit chat. That is not my forte, so I nod and smile along, still feeling like an absolute king for having her in my arms.

Something tickles in my mind though, like I can feel eyes burning in the back of my head. Turning around, the only person I recognize is Old Ethel, but she's not looking at me. She's not looking at me so intently, it's like she *was* looking at me and is trying really hard not to anymore.

I kiss Noelle on the cheek. "Be right back, goddess. Don't skate off anywhere."

She pats my ass as I stroll over to the demoness who owes me $500.

"Jaromar." She looks me up and down in that caustic, assessing way she did the first day, the way that pricked my insecurities. Despite being bare-chested with all my scars on display, I don't feel that same reaction anymore. Her fingers fan out toward me, flames flickering on each tip for a beat. "You have my keys? I assume you're checking out early."

I smile. She's hoping I forgot about our little wager.

"I still have two and a half days. I'll need to go up and get my things once the road is clear. It's a lovely cabin, by the way. Five stars."

"They cleared the road hours ago." She scoffs and shrugs. "And thanks, I guess."

"Turns out Noelle is pretty fond of me," I say, leaning closer to her, waiting for her to catch on. "I guess I'll be sticking around."

Her blood-red, glowing eyes slide back to me. "So you're a local now?"

I puff up my chest, smug that I managed to get the town's pretty librarian to fall for me. "Looks like it."

The demoness's grin blooms, a half-moon shape full of sharp teeth. She sticks out her hand again with the same flourish, the golden flames slightly brighter. "That'll be $500."

"What?" I sputter. "You owe me!"

"We bet on whether Noelle would or wouldn't date an outsider, didn't we?" Her expression morphs to mock innocence in a flash that would earn her an Academy Award.

"We bet on whether she would or wouldn't date *me*!" I point at my chest.

"When you were an outsider." Her brows furrow, looking at me like I'm slow in the head. "That was the only detail I remember specifying."

Her fingers crook, as if waiting for her money and annoyed I haven't coughed it up yet. This is some shady fine print finagling. These old demonesses, I swear. They can talk a man out of his underwear in two seconds flat. As it happens, that's all I'm down to.

"It's a draw," I say, mostly bluffing, hoping I get out of this with nothing lost.

Her open hand snaps closed as she clicks her fingers, pulling a cigarette from her front pocket and lighting it. She studies me for a moment with the ghost of a smile before waving it at me dismissively. "Seems fair."

I back away slowly, a little stunned. I think she just talked me out of the $500 she owed me and made me feel grateful about it.

I find Noelle and hug her from behind. She's chatting with a short human lady who looks familiar. I whisper in her ear, "Remind me never to make a bet with Old Ethel again."

"Silly goose." Noelle looks back at me with an amused grin, patting my forearm. "No one gets anything over on her. She *never* makes a bet she won't win."

I glance back at the old demoness, now standing with a group of other Devout. Her eyes glow the same shade as the end of her lit cigarette, and she watches me and Noelle with a soft expression I don't think I've ever seen, definitely not when I was a little shit stealing candy from her on my way to the library after school.

Candy I'd always give to Noelle. Did she know, even back then?

She nods her head at me, like she's not upset in the least that I stole her candy, that I made a dumb wager with her, or that Noelle and I ended up together. Almost like she saw it coming all along.

Surely not. I narrow my eyes but give her a slight nod in return. It's always best to be respectful where demonesses are involved.

I kiss a path down Noelle's neck. "Happy New Year, love."

"The happiest," she sighs.

This is our new beginning. No more taking stock of the years that separated us, the days flying by, or the hours and minutes to make a final countdown.

Our future starts now. There are no timelines to a love story, only the next chapter.

Acknowledgements

Lark and Lucy, I am forever lucky to have created such this special little world with you. Your support and friendship makes this whole writing thing way more fun than I ever thought it could be.

To our beta readers, I cannot thank you enough, but I'll continue to try. This interconnected series was intimidating to execute, and we couldn't have cross-checked and typo-hunted and shined these babies up without you. Your impact was immense. So thank you, thank you, thank you to Mallory, Emily, Luna, Amy, Raluca, Trisha, Andria, Barb, Meagan, Melissa, May, Kenzie, Diana, Jessica, Amber, Sara, Anna, Peggy, Ahren, Tia, Andria, Jenny, Raj, and MJ. I hope this story will always have a small part of your heart, just as you will always have mine.

Special thanks to the artists included in this book: Brina Boyle, Luna Wolff, Daniel, Sali, and H Holden. One of my favorite parts of being an indie author is partnering with incredible indie artists. Shout out to the other creative souls who made art of Rom and Noelle you can find on my website and social media – Lianne Peterson, Sadie Sparkle, Chela, Lucy, and Laura. I adore you all.

Last, thanks to our amazing ARC team. You are the beating heart of the literary world, and I hope you never forget it. We appreciate you so much.

Author's Note

Thank you for spending your valuable time reading this little love story. It will always be so surreal that I can share my imagination with you in this way.

I encourage you to support your local library. Even something as simple as getting a library card helps. In light of the recent rash of book banning, as Rom says, "What the library needs . . . is support to grow stronger, not a place [it] has to shrink to fit."

Sign up for my newsletter to get access to a top-secret, sexy epilogue of Noelle and Rom as well as regular updates on future stories.

Playlist

I chose one song per chapter! Hope you enjoy.

1. Busy Earnin' by Jungle

2. Good Days by SZA

3. numb myself by Corbon Amodio

4. There's No Way by Lauv & Julia Michaels

5. Damage Gets Done by Hozier, Brandi Carlile

6. Letters To Ghosts by Lucie Silvas

7. Stick Season by Noah Kahan

8. Taxi by EXES

9. Home by Edith Whiskers

10. Falling by Mansionair

11. Meet Me in the Woods by Lord Huron

12. ur so pretty by Wasia Project

13. Sugar by Sleep Token

14. Sleep Deprivation Song by Chance Peña

15. Francesca by Hozier